The LAST D

The LAST DOG on EARTH

DANIEL EHRENHAFT

DELACORTE PRESS

Published by
Delacorte Press
an imprint of
Random House Children's Books
a division of Random House, Inc.
New York, New York

Produced by 17th Street Productions
an Alloy, Inc. company
151 West 26th Street
New York, New York 10011

Visit us on the Web! www.randomhouse.com/teens

Educators and librarians, for a variety of teaching tools, visit us at www.randomhouse.com/teachers

Cataloging-in-Publication Data is available from the Library of Congress.

ISBN: 0-385-73005-5 (trade)
ISBN: 0-385-90083-X (lib. bdg.)

The text of this book is set in 11.5 point Adobe Caslon.

Cover design by Amy Beadle

Printed in the United States of America

February 2003

10 9 8 7 6 5 4 3 2 1

BVG

For Cecily and Josh

Prologue
THE SHE-PUP

Before the sickness, the pack had always hunted at night. The darkness gave it power. At night, the pack could be one—a stealthy, many-headed beast: dozens of eyes, hundreds of sharp teeth bared for an attack. The creatures who hid or burrowed underground during the day would emerge in the shadows, and the damp air would ripen with their mingled scents: beaver, chipmunk, deer—all nearby, all feasts for the taking.

Tonight, as always, the forest was full of possibilities. But tonight the pack was too weak to hunt. The sickness had all but destroyed it.

The she-pup stood beside Mother at the mouth of the cave, whining softly. The emptiness in her belly was a sharp, gnawing pain. Mother had been still for days. She had to start stalking prey again—not only for her own survival, but for the rest of the pack . . . and mostly for the she-pup and her brother, White Paws. Both were only six months old. Too young to fend for themselves.

At last, Mother growled. She shook herself and stretched. The wait was over. The she-pup's belly rumbled in anticipation. She sat, every sense focused on Mother's movement. Foam dripped from Mother's mouth. Her legs buckled. There was a foul odor coming off her, but the she-pup ignored it. She wagged her tail and rubbed against her mother's body, welcoming her back to the world of the living.

Mother turned to her. Their eyes locked. The puppy's tail fell still.

Mother's eyes were not her own. They were clouded, dull, seeing but not knowing. A thousand generations of canine instinct flowed through the puppy's veins, and they all boiled down to a single command: Run.

She darted out of the cave.

Mother lunged at her. Her jaws closed within inches of the she-pup's tail. The she-pup sprinted through the forest as fast as her starved body would carry her. Mother followed close on her heels, barking. The sound was savage, ferocious. Mud flew; twigs snapped; the puppy lost her footing several times. But Mother lost her footing as well. She staggered more than she ran.

Eventually, the she-pup grew too weak to continue. She whirled to face Mother, her heart pounding. Mother closed in on her with great wheezing gasps.

And then she collapsed.

The puppy hesitated. She took a few tentative steps forward, sniffing. There was a new scent in the air now. . . .

Like fear, it had been burned into her memory since before she was born. But she'd also encountered it firsthand—whenever she'd hunted at Mother's side for a night's meal.

It was the scent of death.

Incident Report
Redmont County Sheriff's Office
June 15

Officers Vasquez and Roper, responding to a domestic disturbance call, went to 719 Nakootick Way. At the scene, homeowner Michelle Thompson reported that her Labrador retriever, Jellybean, had attempted to maul her eleven-year-old son. "He just went crazy. I've never seen anything like it," Mrs. Thompson stated. The boy was unharmed, but when the dog continued its violent and aggressive behavior, Mrs. Thompson and her son vacated the premises.

Officers determined that the dog was still inside the house, and loud barking and thudding noises indicated it was still agitated. Officer Roper, formerly of the Portland canine unit, entered the house in an attempt to soothe the animal, at which point the animal began to pursue Officer Roper. In the course of evading attack, Officer Roper jumped through a picture window. When the dog came through the window in pursuit, Officer Vasquez was forced to shoot. A veterinarian was summoned and the dog was pronounced dead at the scene at 6:18 P.M.

PART I
JUNE 20-21

CHAPTER ONE

"You know what the Wallaces' dog can do?" Robert asked. He slapped the steering wheel. "He can fetch his own leash when he wants to go for a walk. Can you believe that? Otis fetches his own leash!"

Robert had an annoying habit of slapping the steering wheel while he was talking and driving at the same time. Logan hated that.

Logan Moore hated a lot of things.

Mom said that *hate* was a strong word and that Logan shouldn't use it. Logan didn't agree. If *hate* was a strong word, then that was fine by him. If there had been a stronger word, he'd probably have used that one. In fact, hating was such a big part of his life that he kept a running list of all the things he hated.

The list changed from day to day. It could change from hour to hour, even. Sometimes it was bigger, sometimes smaller; sometimes it was just one word—*Robert*—so Logan never wrote the list down. He kept it in his head, where he kept everything else that mattered.

Right now the list read as follows:

THINGS I HATE

1. Being in the car with Mom and Robert
2. Listening to Robert jabber on and on and *never shut up* about the Wallaces' dog
3. The Wallaces

4. Their dog
5. The name Otis
6. Devon Wallace
7. Being angry

The list always ended the same way, because even on a beautiful June afternoon—with summer vacation just starting and the sun blazing and the wind whipping through the open car window—Logan could count on being angry for one reason or another. At the very least, he could always be angry that Mom had married Robert, whose pockmarked face looked like the surface of an asteroid and whose mission in life was to be the All-Knowing Dictator of Everything. Logan could also be angry that his father had run off when Logan was seven and was now living the high life somewhere in the boondocks in a mansion he'd built by himself that probably had a hot tub and a trampoline—but Logan wouldn't know because his father had never invited him to the place and never would. (Not that Logan even wanted to go.) And of course he could be angry about being angry all the time, since it was a lousy way to feel.

But Logan had gotten used to all that sort of stuff. He'd *had* to get used to it, or else he'd go crazy. And then, who knew what could happen? He might turn violent. He might turn to crime. Then he would end up being one of those kids you see on talk shows: the kids whose heinous behavior *proves* to the studio audience that teenagers are, indeed, very evil—and isn't it high time we did something about it?

Today Logan was just angry because Robert had burst into his room without knocking. *Again.* Then he'd torn the place apart, searching for the TV remote control. *Again.* He couldn't find it, of course, because Logan didn't have it. But that didn't stop him from throwing all Logan's stuff all over the place . . . his clothes, his books, *everything*—even the lousy baseball mitt that he never used because it was so stiff that it felt like concrete, and besides, there was nobody to play catch with, anyway.

Then Robert told him to clean up the mess.

And on top of all that, Mom and Robert were dragging him to the Wallaces' Summer Kickoff Barbecue for the eighty billionth time. Logan would rather have his eyes poked out with a sharp stick. He'd rather be hurled into a pit full of poisonous snakes. He'd rather do *anything* than be stuck in the same place as both Robert and Devon Wallace.

But there was no point in dwelling on what he'd rather be doing.

Every year, the Wallaces hosted the same Summer Kickoff Barbecue. Everybody in Pinewood was invited. That was the Pinewood spirit. Pinewood was the lame housing tract in the lame town where they all lived—that being Newburg, Oregon, otherwise known as Lameville, USA. And every year, the star attraction of the barbecue was Devon Wallace, the King of Lameness himself.

Devon was fourteen, just like Logan. They'd been in the same class since they were five. They were both going to start ninth grade at the same high school in the fall. Given Logan's luck, they would probably go to the same college, work at the same office, and end up buried in the same cemetery, too.

For the longest time, Mom and Robert had been putting up a fight to make Logan become better friends with Devon. It didn't take a genius to see why. From an adult point of view, Devon was perfect. He was a perfectly adequate student. He had perfect blond hair and perfect teeth. He was one of those kids who looked as if he belonged in a toothpaste commercial. He played about a zillion different sports, too, including soccer and water polo—yes, water polo—all perfectly.

Logan, on the other hand, had messy brown hair and a crooked smile (which most people never saw). People said he looked like his mother. Why, he wasn't sure. Mom was a middle-aged woman. How could he possibly look like her? He and Mom were both skinny, though, and they had blue eyes, which was probably what people were talking about.

As far as school went, he hated it and skipped whenever he could. And when it came to sports, he was decent at minigolf, but not much else. He liked to go hiking. But you couldn't *beat* anybody at hiking.

In other words, he didn't rate so high on the perfection scale.

So it was natural that his mother and stepfather would want him to hang out with Devon Wallace. They were hoping that some of Devon's perfection would rub off on him. Unfortunately, Mom and Robert missed what every single other adult also seemed to miss about Devon—namely, that he was an ass.

He was the worst kind of ass, too: a mean one. When adults weren't around, Devon spent all his time bragging or picking on other kids—especially if they were younger. He treated Logan as if he were an idiot because Logan didn't get good grades. As if grades had anything to do with how smart you really were.

It figured, though. The lamest people always made it their business to get good grades. Then they made it their business to find out what kind of grades everybody else got and make fun of them if they did badly.

". . . and I'm sure Devon has a great time with Otis," Robert was saying. "Labradors are the best dogs on earth."

Logan couldn't believe it. Robert was *still* yammering on about the Wallaces' dog. He hadn't stopped since they'd pulled out of the driveway. He'd barely even taken a breath.

"Not all Labradors," Mom said.

Robert scowled at her. "What do you mean?"

"It's just . . . remember what I told you about Michelle Thompson? You know, my friend from Redmont?"

"No," Robert said. "What about her?"

Mom sighed. "Last week, her son was playing with their new Lab. And the dog attacked him. The poor kid needed twelve stitches. Apparently she even had to hire somebody to come . . . well, to come take care of the dog."

Robert snorted. "The kid probably provoked it. I had a Lab growing up. They're the best dogs on earth," he repeated, as if saying it twice somehow made it more true.

Mom sighed again, then shrugged. "You're probably right."

"Of course I'm right," Robert said. "Anyway, playing with a dog is a lot less dangerous than sitting alone in your room all day, playing with broken household appliances." His dark eyes met Logan's in the rearview mirror. "Speaking of which, what's in that bag?"

Logan blinked. "Huh?"

Robert glared at him. "Hello? Earth to Logan? Anybody home? I want to know what's in your backpack."

"Nothing," Logan said.

"It can't be *nothing*. I can see that *something's* in it."

"Robert," Mom said. "Please. Keep your eyes on the road."

"I just want to know what kind of trouble your son's got in that bag," Robert said.

"Nothing," Logan repeated. He wasn't lying. Not technically. There was a very good chance that the device in the bag beside him—his latest invention, the Logan Moore Master Remote Control, or LMMRC—wouldn't work. If something didn't work, it didn't count. Therefore, it meant nothing. It *was* nothing.

Robert's eyes kept flashing to the mirror. "It's trouble, isn't it?"

"Actually, it's supposed to stop trouble," Logan said. The LMMRC was big enough that even Robert would have a hard time losing it.

"Don't be smart," Robert snapped.

As the All-Knowing Dictator of Everything, Robert loved dishing out important-sounding commands—most of which began with the word *don't*. His favorite: "Don't turn this into a production, Logan."

"It's a master remote control," Logan explained reluctantly. "I made it from that old model airplane control panel."

"Whoa, whoa, wait a second here," Robert said, grimacing. "You mean the model airplane control panel we got you for Christmas? Logan, did you break that?"

"Um, well . . . ," Logan said. "I, uh, changed it a little."

Robert laughed. He turned to Logan's mom. "You hear that? He *changed* it a little. Translation: There's another seventy bucks down the toilet. Remind me about this when December rolls around."

"Robert," Mom said tersely. "Please. Watch the road."

"It was mine," Logan muttered. "Why can't I do what I want with my own stuff?" He'd never asked for the model airplane, anyway. Robert had bought it because *he* wanted it. Because he'd had one when he was growing up.

"You know what your problem is, Logan?" Robert said. "You're ungrateful. You don't appreciate anything I try to do for you—"

"Please," Mom begged. "Both of you! Let's not get into it now. We're almost to the barbecue."

"I'm telling you, Marianne," Robert said, as if Logan weren't there. "The kid needs to shape up. He's heading for trouble. I still say we should have sent him to that camp, like Powell said. They'd have taught him some discipline. Some respect."

"Maybe next year," Logan's mother murmured. "When he's older."

Logan could feel the muscles in his neck tightening. He turned his head and stared out the window. "That camp" was the Blue Mountain Camp for Boys. It had been founded by an ex-marine and was supposed to whip kids into shape by treating them like soldiers in a boot camp. Or prisoners. Logan had looked it up online. The picture showed a bunch of barrackslike huts surrounded by a tall cyclone fence with razor wire at the top. *That* was where Robert wanted to send him.

Nice, he thought.

Robert turned onto the Wallaces' block and pulled up to the curb. The barbecue was already in full swing. The street was jammed with cars. Logan could hear the faint strains of music from behind the Wallaces' big, perfect, beautiful house—the kind of cheesy light rock music that only adults who lived in big, perfect, beautiful houses seemed to listen to. There were bright balloons hanging from the tree on the Wallaces' wide front lawn and a hand-painted sign:

COME AROUND BACK! NO PARTY POOPERS ALLOWED!

"You know what?" Logan said. "Maybe I should just wait in the car. I don't think I'm allowed inside."

"What in God's name are you talking about?" Robert demanded.

But Logan didn't feel like explaining. Because if he did, Robert would get angry. He'd probably have a heart attack. And that would be great at first, because Robert would clutch at his chest and choke out, "Help me! Help me!" . . . but then he would grab Logan's neck in a final horror-movie moment and strangle him, and they would stare at each other, eyes bulging, until they both died—because the most fiendish horror-movie villains always manage to get in one last terrible crime before they get killed.

Which wouldn't be so great.

So Logan just shrugged.

Robert turned off the engine and pulled the key from the ignition. He leaned over the seat and looked Logan in the eye.

"Don't turn this into a production, Logan," he said.

Statement given by Rudy Stagg to Sheriff Van Wyck of the Redmont County, Oregon Sheriff's Office on June 20

My name is Rudy Stagg. I am forty-two years old, and I have lived in Redmont my whole life. I am a home security consultant. I also run a dog-training business. I train dogs for home security.

For the record, I want to state that I did absolutely nothing wrong. I shot and killed the dog this morning because the dog was endangering human beings. In my judgment deadly force was necessary. As every officer in this town knows, I am licensed to carry a firearm. I own a registered .357 Colt Magnum.

Derek Colby called me because his Rottweilers were acting strange. Now, these were dogs that I knew and trained myself, so I went out to see what was wrong. When I got there, one of the dogs was actually attacking him. I barely managed to get the shots off in time. The other dog was already dead when we went inside. We took it to a vet to be examined.

This isn't the first time I've heard about a dog going nuts recently. Another client of mine, James Tetford, called me four days ago to ask me to train up a new Doberman for him. The one he bought from me last year was mauled to death by a neighbor's dog. Weird thing is, the neighbor's dog was some little weenie thing. Beagle? Spaniel? Something like that.

And I also heard on my police-band radio about that Lab up on Nakootick Way that your officers had to put down. Seems to me there's some kind of new dog bug going around.

Killing dogs is not my profession. But I stand by my constitutional right to bear arms and use them when necessary.

Thank you.

CHAPTER TWO

The Wallaces' Summer Kickoff Barbecue was even worse than Logan had expected.

Fortunately, nobody in the backyard even really noticed that he was there. The adults were all standing in little clusters by the pool, slurping beer and laughing. Devon Wallace was bullying every single kid into playing Ping-Pong with him, even the eight-year-olds. Robert sat on a folding lawn chair next to the gas grill, where Mr. Wallace was flipping burgers in an apron and a white chef's hat. Judging from the way Robert was looking at Mr. Wallace, you'd think the guy had just discovered the cure for cancer.

Logan wasn't surprised. It was all part of Robert's act. He had this annoying habit of pretending to be interested in whatever Mr. Wallace had to say, no matter how boring it was. Mr. Wallace could be talking about cleaning his pool or some other garbage that would make most normal people want to take a nap, but Robert would just sit there with this *look* on his face . . . and Logan couldn't help wondering if he'd spent hours in the mirror practicing it—the *concerned* look, the *serious* look: eyes focused, forehead wrinkled, as if to say, "Oh, yes, I completely understand why cleaning your pool is such an important subject, and I have some important opinions of my own!"

Then speak up! Logan always wanted to tell him. *We're all very curious!*

It was obvious why Robert tried so hard. Mr. Wallace had everything Robert wanted: a lot of money, a big house, a swimming pool, and a perfect son. So Robert probably figured that if he listened carefully enough (or at least pretended to listen), he'd discover the key to getting all those things himself. It was pretty sad, if you really thought about it.

Well, actually it wasn't *that* sad, because it was sort of funny, in a way. The thing was, Robert would always get bored with Mr. Wallace after about five minutes and start stuffing his face with food. Then he'd get bored with *that*. Back and forth, back and forth. That was the general pattern of the Summer Kickoff Barbecue. Mostly Logan just stood off to the side and watched Robert at work: pigging out, phony-baloney, pigging out, phony-baloney. . . .

"I thought Outward Bound was for troublemakers," Robert was saying. He grabbed an open bag of potato chips from the table beside him and stuffed some into his mouth.

Mr. Wallace shook his head. "Not at all. It teaches valuable life skills. Teamwork. Survival. Self-motivation." He laughed. "Not like Devon needs to learn that kind of thing. I'm sure he'll be running the whole program by the end of it."

"Going was all Devon's idea?" Robert asked.

"Yes, it was," Mr. Wallace said proudly. He stopped flipping burgers for a moment and glanced at Robert. "You know, you might want to think about something like Outward Bound for Logan."

Robert grimaced. "We *have* thought about it," he said. "Actually, Logan's guidance counselor recommended one of those special boot camps. You know, for troubled kids."

Uh-oh. As quickly as he could, Logan ducked behind some bushes at the edge of the patio. He didn't want to hear anything more about his guidance counselor, Mr. Powell. During the past year, the school had made him have "sessions" with Mr. Powell twice a week. Mr. Powell would sit there and try to get Logan to explain why he cut school so often and didn't make any effort in his classes, and Logan would sit there and not answer. Wasn't it obvious?

"Boot camp would be perfect for a nonverbal type like you," Mr. Powell had told him.

A nonverbal type. Logan couldn't believe people actually talked like that. *It's not that I'm nonverbal,* he'd almost said. *It's just that I have nothing to say to* you.

Whatever. School was out for the summer. He wouldn't have to see Mr. Powell again until September. Besides, right now he had more important things to worry about, like testing the Logan Moore Master Remote Control.

He bent down and slung his backpack off his shoulders, then gingerly removed the LMMRC. A smile spread across his face. Even if the thing didn't work, at least it *looked* cool. It was heavy and black—about the size of a shoe box—with two long silver antennae sticking out from the front of it in a V shape, like an insect's head. Come to think of it, the big dial in the middle was sort of like a nose. And the big red button could be a pimple. Or a wart. Yeah . . . in fact, the whole device looked more like the face of some freakish, prehistoric bug than like a souped-up remote control. Which made sense, in a way. There was an electronic brain inside. A brain with telepathic powers.

If it worked. But Logan was pretty sure—

Something brushed up against his legs. He swiveled around and found himself nose to nose with a chocolate brown Labrador.

Otis. Logan frowned.

The dog was panting. Logan could smell his breath. It wasn't very pleasant.

"Shoo, boy," Logan whispered. He stood up straight. "Go on. Shoo. Get out of here—"

"Hey, Logan! What are you doing?"

Logan's shoulders sagged. Just his luck: Devon Wallace was coming his way.

Devon was all sweaty from Ping-Pong, but every blond hair was still perfectly in place. He sneered at the LMMRC.

"Whatcha got there?" he asked.

"Nothing," Logan mumbled. He was beginning to wish he'd never opened his backpack.

Otis's tail started wagging.

"What is it, some kind of remote control?" Devon asked.

"Something like that," Logan said. "I was just—"

"Here, let me see it," Devon interrupted. He snatched the LMMRC from Logan's grasp. "What's it supposed to do?" He pushed the red button and flicked the dial.

"Nothing," Logan said.

Devon shoved the LMMRC back into Logan's hands. "I bet I could whip your butt in Ping-Pong," he said.

Logan shrugged. "I'm sure you could."

"You want to play me?"

"Not really."

"Come on," Devon said. He grinned. "I've whipped everybody else's butt. You're the only one who hasn't played me yet."

Otis started licking one of Devon's sweaty legs. His big tongue made a slurping noise.

"I don't really like Ping-Pong," Logan said.

"Probably because you stink at it," Devon said.

"Probably," Logan agreed. He thought for a minute. "Actually, I'd say definitely. That's definitely why I don't like it."

"So you really don't want to play me?" Devon asked. He sounded annoyed.

"What's the point?" Logan said. "We both know you're going to win, right? Here, I'll tell you what. Let's tell people that we just played and you creamed me. How's that? You can tell everyone here that I didn't even score a single point. I'll go along with whatever you say."

For what seemed like a long time, Devon just stared at Logan, as if he'd answered in Swahili. Then he stalked off.

"Weirdo," he muttered under his breath.

Logan almost laughed. Guys like Devon never knew what to do with anyone who didn't accept some dumb challenge. They counted on you being just like them, needing to win. They needed to humiliate you in public, even if the whole world already knew that you stank. Winning was the only thing that counted.

That was weird.

On the other hand, Logan could guess why Devon felt he had to win all the time. His parents never shut up about how great he was— at sports and pretty much everything else. So he probably felt some sort of obligation to whip everybody, as if he had to keep living up to what his parents said. You sort of had to feel a little sorry for him.

Sort of.

Logan scanned the backyard for something he could test the LMMRC on. There was nothing on the lawn by the Ping-Pong table, just Devon looking sulky . . . nothing by the pool, just a bunch of dumb kids splashing around . . . nothing by the grill—

Aha. The stereo.

It was perched on the patio wall, right by the sliding glass doors that led to the kitchen. A slender black remote lay beside it. The radio was still tuned to that cheesy adult rock station.

As quietly as he could, Logan crept across the back of the patio, bending low so Robert and Mr. Wallace wouldn't notice him—and zeroed in on a row of potted plants about ten feet from the stereo. He tiptoed the last few steps and crouched behind the leaves, parting them with the antennae. Then he flicked the dial to S (for *stereo*) and pressed the red button.

Nothing happened.

He pressed it once more.

Still nothing.

Hmmm. Okay. He reminded himself not to be too discouraged. There were bound to be a few kinks in any invention. Take his last masterpiece—the LMSPWW (the Logan Moore Superpowerful Weed Whacker). It had had to be modified several times before it did what it was supposed to do. In fact, he'd been forced to take apart the entire motor and rebuild it twice before he got it right. Anyway, the Wallaces' stereo might use some kind of special frequency.

Just for kicks, he flicked the dial to GDO (*garage door opener*) and pressed the button a third time.

The music stopped.

It works! Logan bit his lip to keep from saying the words out loud.

Mr. Wallace and Robert frowned at the stereo.

Logan pressed the button again. The music kicked back in.

Mr. Wallace and Robert exchanged a puzzled glance. They both shrugged and turned back to the grill.

Logan grinned. Now he was getting somewhere. Still, it was one thing to turn a stereo on and off; it was another actually to *control* it. He flicked a switch marked Volume, then gave the dial below it a twist.

A piercing, high-pitched whistle exploded from the speakers.

Logan flinched. *Yikes.* That was really loud. It sounded like a fire alarm.

Mr. Wallace dropped his spatula. He clamped his hands over his ears and scowled at Robert. Robert clamped his hands over his ears, too. Otis barked. His ears stiffened.

"What's going on?" Mr. Wallace shouted.

Robert shook his head. Otis was barking wildly now.

Logan twisted the volume knob on the LMMRC back to zero. The speakers crackled a little, but that was it. Not good. Everybody was holding their hands over their ears and making faces at the stereo. Their cheeks were all scrunched up like dried fruit.

"Come on, come on," Logan muttered. He jabbed at the red button. Nothing happened.

Otis's bark turned into a howl: *"Ahhh-oooo."* He started chasing his tail, running in tight, crazy circles on the lawn.

"Turn it off !" Devon yelled from across the yard. "Turn it off!"

Mr. Wallace strode toward the stereo, hands still tight over his ears. At the same moment, Otis came out of his circle and started for the patio. He barreled straight into Mr. Wallace's legs. Mr. Wallace stumbled and crashed to the lawn. His chef's hat fell off his head.

"Ahhh-oooo!" Otis howled.

Logan giggled. He knew he shouldn't, but he couldn't help it.

Otis lunged at the stereo.

Logan's jaw dropped. The dog's brown body hurtled through

the air and slammed right into the CD player, knocking it off the patio wall. The big silver box bounced on the flagstones with a metallic thud. The speaker cables jerked. Logan winced, squeezing his eyes shut. *Please don't break. Please don't—*

The whistling stopped.

Logan opened his eyes.

The backyard fell silent. Well, almost. Otis still hadn't calmed down. In fact, he seemed to have worked himself into a brand-new frenzy—racing around and snorting. Mr. Wallace sat on the lawn, looking dazed.

"All right, everybody stay calm!" Devon yelled. He ran alongside the pool. "I'll handle the dog!" He waved his arms. "Bad dog! Heel, boy! Heel!"

Otis bolted straight for him.

Devon dropped to one knee at the pool's edge and pointed toward the ground. "I said *heel*," he growled. "Right now."

Otis didn't even slow down. He crashed into Devon and pushed him off balance. For a moment, Devon teetered over the clear blue water—then he toppled in. *Splash!*

Everybody gasped.

Logan burst out laughing. Otis looked pleased with himself, as if he'd just pulled off a really neat trick—even neater than fetching his own leash. He kept right on running, around and around the pool. His tail wagged.

Devon's hair looked like a stringy blond mop. It hung in his face and dripped on his drenched clothes as he hauled himself out of the water.

"Logan! What are you doing?"

Uh-oh. Robert had spotted him behind the plants.

"What do you have there?" Robert demanded, his face reddening.

"It's . . . uh, that remote control thingy I was telling you about," Logan said. He stood up and glanced at Mr. Wallace. Now he felt bad. The poor guy was hunched over the fallen CD player, examining it very carefully, the way a doctor would examine a patient. There was a grass stain on the seat of his khaki shorts.

"*You* did this," Robert sputtered. "Didn't you? Didn't you? Answer me!"

"I think I did," Logan admitted. He stepped out from behind the plants and cleared his throat. "Sorry."

Mr. Wallace lifted the CD player and set it back on the patio wall. He forced a strained smile. "That's okay, Logan," he said. "I'm sure you didn't blow my stereo speakers *on purpose*." He emphasized the last two words, as if to tell Logan that he didn't really mean what he was saying.

"If anything's broken, I'll pay for it," Logan said.

"Pay for it?" Robert asked. "With what? When you say *you'll* pay for it, you really mean *I'll* pay for it. You think this is funny, don't you?"

Logan didn't answer. His face was hot. Everybody was staring at him.

"You know, I think it's okay," Mr. Wallace said. Now he sounded embarrassed. "The speaker cables just got ripped out. Really, Robert. It's not that big a deal. They make these stereos to withstand a lot of abuse."

"Can I take a look at it?" Logan offered. "If it's broken, maybe I could fix it."

"Don't you think you've done enough damage for one day?" Robert asked. He planted himself between Logan and Mr. Wallace and folded his arms across his chest. "If you think I'm going to let you get within five feet of the Wallaces' stereo, think again."

"But I didn't mean to break it," Logan argued. "I'm just trying to help."

"Help?" Robert sniffed. "That's a first."

Logan's jaw tightened. His eyes darted around the backyard, searching for his mother. Why was Robert even getting involved? *(a)* It was an accident, and *(b)* it was none of his business. If this was a real problem, Mom should be getting involved, not Robert. Logan was *her* son. Besides, she knew that if Logan said he wanted to help, he meant it.

But Mom was nowhere to be seen.

Logan shook his head. She'd probably slunk inside the Wallaces' house as soon as Robert started ranting. That was classic Mom: Run and hide when things start getting ugly. It was classic all around. The whole sequence of events really couldn't get any *more* classic.

"Let's just forget about it, huh?" Mr. Wallace suggested. He picked his chef's hat and spatula up off the patio, then walked back over to the grill. "Looks like these burgers are almost ready, anyway. It's chow time." He wiped the spatula on his apron.

Robert shook his head. He turned his back on Logan.

"Now I've got to go change," Devon yelled, to nobody in particular. He marched toward the house, his wet sneakers squelching on the cement. "This is great. Just great."

Otis trailed after him. He finally seemed to have calmed down.

As Devon walked past him, Logan cleared his throat. "Sorry."

Devon shot him a venomous glance, then slammed the door behind him. Otis jumped backward as the metal screening nearly hit him on the nose.

"I don't know what his problem is," Robert said to Mr. Wallace. "The kid's got serious issues. He starts trouble wherever he goes."

The kid.

Logan repeated the words to himself. *The kid.* Not *Logan.* Not his name. Not as if he weren't standing right behind Robert, not as if he couldn't hear every single thing Robert was saying. No. *The kid.*

Mr. Wallace shrugged. He dished a couple of burgers onto a plate. Otis trotted over and sat beside him, panting and staring intently at the meat.

"It's his father," Robert continued. "That's where he gets it."

Now Logan almost felt like laughing. What could his father possibly have to do with what he was like? What could his father have to do with anything at all? Logan barely even knew the guy.

Robert truly was a moron. He never failed to outstupid himself.

"Maybe you should think about getting Logan a dog," Mr. Wallace said. He reached down and scratched Otis behind the ears. "I tell you, training Otis really taught Devon the value of discipline and responsibility. . . ."

Logan had heard just about enough. He turned and trudged around the house to the car. He'd just wait there until it was time to go. If Robert believed that the key to solving all of Logan's problems was to turn him into the next Devon Wallace, then that was fine. Logan just didn't want to be around to listen to it.

Which, in a way, was the main reason he hadn't wanted to come to the whole Summer Kickoff Barbecue in the first place.

E-mail exchange between Sheriff Van Wyck and Dr. Harold Marks, chief of the Portland University Research Center for Infectious Diseases

To: hmarks@portlanduniversity.edu
From: vanwyck@redmontsheriff.org
Date: June 20
Subject: A DOG DISEASE

Dear Dr. Marks,

My name is John Van Wyck. I'm the sheriff of Redmont, a small town about a hundred miles south of Portland. Your name came up in our database as somebody who might know about a disease that's been affecting the dogs in our area. The symptoms are like rabies, but they also include loss of body control and sleepiness. Dr. Claudia Juarez, a local veterinarian, autopsied two of the dogs, but the results were inconclusive. I have asked her to forward her notes to you in hopes that you'll find something she missed.

A local dog trainer has been stirring up a fuss by shooting these dogs, and we want to put an end to the shootings if we can. Any help you could give us would be greatly appreciated. Also, the database came up with a Dr. Craig Westerly, but he doesn't seem to be listed in your university's current directory. Has he moved to another university? Please let us know. Thanks.

To: vanwyck@redmontsheriff.org
From: DR. HAROLD MARKS<hmarks@portlanduniversity.edu>
Date: June 20
Subject: Re: A DOG DISEASE

mr. van wyck:

thanks for getting in touch with me. it's important that we learn about outbreaks such as this one, and i appreciate your contacting us. i'll look into it immediately. i wouldn't bother trying to find craig westerly, however, because he no longer works at any university. he was let go several years ago. i doubt he even works in the field anymore. we'll handle it from here. i'll be in touch.

CHAPTER
THREE

The prisoner was ready for execution.

Dr. Craig Westerly liked to think of his laboratory rats as prisoners. Somehow that made it easier for him to put them out of their misery—as if they'd been jailed for committing some terrible crime. He didn't give them names, either. This particular rat was simply known as F-6. He was fat and gray and very, very sick.

F stood for *flu*. Six was the number of rats Westerly had used so far in this latest experiment. He was trying to invent a flu vaccine that could be inhaled, like asthma medicine. He wanted to replace flu shots. Nobody liked flu shots. They were painful. They made your arm sore and swollen. Some people even had bad reactions to them and got *sick*. An inhaled flu vaccine would do away with all the pain and swelling and bad reactions.

So much of medicine was really barbaric, when you thought about it. So many of the treatments were practically worse than the diseases they were supposed to cure. In Westerly's opinion, it was because the medical community didn't really care about their patients. They were simply interested in money and fame.

That's why I left it all, Westerly reminded himself. *So I could get out here and work on real science, with no politics to mess it up.*

He told himself that a lot.

Unfortunately, Westerly wasn't having much luck with his

research. He couldn't figure out the right dosage. His rats just kept getting the flu every time they inhaled the vaccine.

"Oh, well," he said. "Guess we'll have to wait and see how F-7 does. Eh, Jasmine?"

Jasmine, his big, lazy golden retriever, sat by his feet on the home laboratory floor, watching as he dumped a pellet of ether into F-6's specially sealed glass tank. Jasmine was seven years old—almost as old in dog years as Westerly was in human years.

The ether quickly put F-6 to sleep. Westerly sighed.

Better luck tomorrow.

He and Jasmine headed out to the back porch.

There was a tree at the edge of Westerly's property that reminded him of a tree he used to climb as a boy. It was an evergreen, tall and cone shaped. The branches were as solid and evenly spaced as the rungs of a ladder. At sunset, if the weather was nice, Westerly would sit on the back porch and watch the tree change colors. Jasmine usually lay beside him. He liked to imagine that she enjoyed watching the tree as much as he did. Truth be told, she mostly slept.

Westerly had fallen in love with the tree the very first moment he laid eyes on it. It was one of the two reasons he'd bought this property. The other reason was that he wanted to be as far away from other people as possible. People were trouble, by and large. His nearest neighbors—an old recluse named Mrs. Hoover and her dog, Daisy—were two miles away, and that was close enough.

On days like today, when the afternoons stretched on and on, the tree would slowly change from green to gold, then to a fiery orange. A few minutes later the branches at the top would come to life with a color that verged on purple—but only for a brief moment. Then the sun would sink behind the mountains on the other side of the valley, and the tree would turn into a skeleton: forbidding and gray. It would stay that way until the next morning.

Climbing the tree had been on Westerly's mind quite a bit recently. During the summer he sometimes felt like a boy again, just watching it. When he was younger, all those years ago, he would have climbed it without a thought. The other kids played baseball or tag, but somehow Westerly always ended up at the top of the old evergreen in the park by his house. There he would dream about traveling in the planes that flew overhead or building a big dome over the entire park to protect it from the rain.

"What do you say, Jazz?" Westerly asked. "Do you think I can climb this one?"

Jasmine was half asleep at his feet. She looked like a fuzzy yellow pillow. She opened her droopy eyes, then sniffed and closed them again.

Westerly smiled. "What's that supposed to mean?"

He loved asking Jasmine questions because he could interpret her answers any way he saw fit. Given her slouchy, uninterested mood, she could be saying, "Come on. Sure, you can climb that tree. You're only fifty years old. That's nothing." Or maybe she was daring him to do it. "Don't waste my time *talking* about climbing the tree. Wake me up when you're at the top." Or maybe she was telling him to give it up. "Are you out of your mind? You can't climb that tree. You're practically a senior citizen."

Westerly smiled. He liked these imaginary conversations. He truly enjoyed Jasmine's company.

He couldn't say that about anyone else.

*   *   *

The sun was well below the mountains when Westerly heard a soft chime from his computer. Somebody was sending him an e-mail. He sighed and opened the rickety porch door for Jasmine.

"Come on, Jazz," he murmured. "Come on, girl. Time to go in."

Jasmine yawned and stretched, then shambled inside and flopped down on the rug next to the desk. Westerly followed her in. The laboratory was dark except for the ghostly blue glow of the computer screen. He sank into his chair and peered at the e-mail in box. The subject line was printed in all capital letters.

NEED A FAVOR

It had been sent by Harold Marks.

Westerly felt like deleting the message without reading it.

Every now and then he heard from Dr. Harold Marks of Portland University. Westerly had worked at Portland University, too, once upon a time. That was how he thought of his career there: "once upon a time"—as if it had happened to somebody else, in a story.

Westerly was quite a bit older than Harold. In fact, Westerly had been Harold's teacher. But from the moment they first met, Harold had treated him with little respect. As a student, he'd immediately started calling Westerly by his first name. *Craig.* Not *Dr. Westerly.* Still, that had never stopped him from taking Dr. Westerly's work and passing it off as his own.

Seven years ago, Harold had been named chief of research at the Center for Infectious Diseases. Westerly couldn't believe it when it happened. The man didn't have an original thought in his head. He wasn't even a good researcher. Westerly didn't want the job for himself; he had no interest in being anyone's boss . . . but he certainly didn't want Harold to be *his* boss. So he protested. But Harold got the job, anyway. And the very first thing he did was fire Westerly.

"I'm sorry," Harold had told him. "You just don't know how to get along with people."

And then Westerly had gone home and told his wife, and a few weeks later she had kicked him out, too. Not as bluntly as Harold— no, instead she'd said in her soft voice, "Maybe you ought to try to talk to Harold about getting your job back." And when he'd argued with her, explaining that there was no way he'd ever go back to Portland, she'd said, "Craig, you're not being reasonable. Can't you just try, for once, to get along with him?" And then later she'd said, "You're not being fair to your family. We can't live like this, Craig!"

So he'd left. Just said "so long" to everything—wife, kid, house, job, life—and come up here.

Maybe Harold was right about me, Westerly thought. *Maybe I don't know how to get along with people.* But getting along with people had nothing to do with science. It could even get in the way of science. How could you concentrate on your research if you were constantly worrying about what other people thought?

Harold's problem was that he cared too much about what other people thought. Of course, the only reason he cared was because he wanted power. As far as Westerly had ever been able to tell, nobody *respected* Harold. But they did fear him—feared his power. Everybody at the university was scared of him. If he couldn't control you, he got rid of you.

Like he got rid of me.

Whatever. That was all in the past. Westerly wasn't bitter anymore.

Life was good here in the Cascade Mountains. He'd built his own laboratory so he could work on any kind of research he wanted. Nobody could betray him or kick him out of their lives—not Harold Marks, not his ex-wife, no one. He was all alone. He could play with Jasmine whenever he felt like it, and wear his pajamas all day long (he was wearing a pair of flannel pj's right now, in fact), and tie his gray hair back in a ponytail—and never, ever, *ever* have to worry about getting along with other people.

He clicked open the e-mail.

we're looking for your research paper on prion diseases. we've been notified that there's been a small outbreak of an unidentified illness among dogs in Redmont, a town in the southern part of the state. it seems to mimic symptoms of both mad cow disease and rabies, very much the way you described in your paper. do you have a copy on file? we can't find it here. if you have it, send it.

Westerly stopped breathing.

In an instant he forgot his annoyance at being disturbed or even being asked to do Harold a favor.

Prion diseases.

Westerly hadn't thought about prion diseases in a long, long time. But if Harold was correct in his suspicions, then a "small outbreak" would be nothing of the sort. It might appear to be small at first, but it wouldn't take long for a few cases to develop into something far more dangerous. Something along the lines of a full-scale epidemic.

Prions were tiny, tiny strands of protein. Generally they were harmless, but every now and then a prion would become misshapen, malformed. The term in the scientific community was *misfolded.* Westerly had always likened these misfolded prions to bad seeds.

Once they found their way inside an animal and planted themselves there, the entire animal turned rotten. Prion diseases weren't like other diseases, which were caused by bacteria or viruses—like the flu, for instance. Misfolded prions couldn't be stopped. Worst of all, misfolded prions were found in food—meat, milk, cheese—almost every kind of food that came from animals.

The good news (if any news could really be considered "good") was that prion diseases weren't directly contagious from one species to another. Mad cow disease, for instance, almost certainly could only be caught by healthy cows from affected ones. But even so, *that* particular epidemic caused near panic in England when scientists discovered that humans could contract a related disease by eating the meat of affected cows. Before mad cow disease was brought under control, people were concerned that the entire population of cows in England would have to be destroyed.

Back at the university, Westerly had tried to prove to Harold how dangerous prion diseases could be. He'd even written a paper on the subject—the very same paper Harold now wanted, in fact. But Harold had never been enthusiastic about it. No prion disease had ever occurred on a large scale in the United States. Humans mostly got it from eating spoiled beef in underdeveloped countries. There was a tribe in New Guinea that had gotten a prion disease called kuru from cannibalism. "There just aren't that many cannibals here in America," Harold used to joke.

Westerly had never found that joke funny.

Then Harold would get serious. "It's not where the grant money is, Craig," he'd say. "Prion diseases are not going to put this university on the map."

"Unless one hits here and we're not prepared for it," Westerly would reply. And Harold would wave his hand and call Westerly Old Gloom-and-Doom.

"I warned him, Jasmine," Westerly said. "Didn't I?"

Jasmine was asleep. Lucky for her.

Westerly leaned back in the chair. He knew he shouldn't panic. After all, Harold was a lousy scientist; he could have misread the data—but if dogs had already died, then the odds were extremely high that they'd caught the disease from infected dog food.

Westerly's eyes flashed to the lab counter on the other side of the room. He drummed his fingers on the desk, staring at the shadowy array of test tubes, osmotic filters, microscopes, and centrifuges. He could test Jasmine's food right now. The equipment was ready. He was one of the few scientists in the country who had such equipment, in fact. Testing for prion diseases was difficult— and given how rare they were, it was hardly worth the effort. Or so most people believed . . . unless there was an outbreak.

But was there?

Yet even as the question squirmed in Westerly's brain, he knew he wouldn't test Jasmine's food. Not tonight. He was too afraid of what he might find. Because if the food *was* infected, he might as well start digging her grave. There was no cure for prion diseases, at least none that had been proven to work. Westerly had a couple of theories on how a cure might be created, of course—but that was all they were: theories. They wouldn't suddenly provide a magic pill that could save a dog's life.

Besides, nobody had ever listened much to his theories, anyway.

Many months had passed since Mother's death. In that time, the sickness had spread. The rest of the pack were gone. Only White Paws and the she-pup remained, left to fend for themselves. They were young, not even a year old. But they were healthy. They were strong. White Paws assumed the role of leader. It was the law of the forest: Those who are strong take charge; those who are weak submit to them or perish.

Yet the she-pup refused to submit to any creature, even her brother.

One night, she took off into the darkness. White Paws tracked her scent over hills and through thick brush, under fallen trees and across puddles. . . .

As he approached the highway, White Paws could smell the horrible odor of the cars, their choking black smog. He could see the fearsome glare of their headlights through the trees. The cars were close—very close. One came to a stop, its roar fading to a low, steady growl. There were other noises, too: strange bumping sounds, the voices of men.

White Paws slithered behind a rock. He could see his sister. He watched as a man scooped her into his arms, then as the car swallowed them both and roared back into the night.

For a long time, White Paws sat by the highway in silence.

But after a while, he began to howl. It was a howl born of a loneliness that every creature of the wild knows—a howl born of the primal understanding of loss.

Letter faxed to Rudy Stagg the night of June 21

Sheila Davis
Associate Editor
The Redmont Daily Standard
170 South Avenue
Redmont, OR 98873

June 21

Dear Mr. Stagg:

I am writing to inquire about the "dog bug" that you discussed in your statement to the police yesterday. I am a reporter for *The Redmont Daily Standard*. I cover the police beat, and Sheriff Van Wyck showed me your statement. It struck me as quite interesting, particularly since I am a dog owner myself.

I think there may be a story here. Do you agree? If so, I'd love to talk further.

Sincerely,
Sheila Davis

PART II
JUNE 22–JULY 3

CHAPTER FOUR

"We're getting you a dog," Robert announced.

Logan didn't look up from his cereal bowl. He'd been expecting something like this. It was Monday morning, and most Mondays began with one of Robert's stupid announcements. (First prize for the stupidest announcement ever: "We're taking away your how-to-build-electronics books, Logan.")

Somehow, Robert always thought that getting something or taking something away would solve all of Logan's problems. It didn't matter how complicated the problems were or if there even *were* any problems. What mattered was solving them in a jiffy. Robert was all about finding a quick fix. The less he had to *deal* with Logan, the better.

Logan was actually relieved. Ever since the barbecue, he'd been worried that Robert would make good on his threat to ship him off to that juvenile delinquent boot camp.

It had been two days since the stereo disaster. Robert had confiscated the LMMRC immediately; no surprise there. But over the weekend, he and Mom had also met for several hushed conferences in the bedroom. With the door locked. And the radio on. That way Logan couldn't hear what they were saying. Which made Logan very nervous.

So when he considered all that, a dog was good news. Sure,

dogs slobbered all over everything and chewed up stuff and barked a lot—but compared to boot camp, they were a piece of cake. They could even come in handy. They could scare off burglars. They could freak out and knock over a stereo at a lame barbecue. Dogs were even given as *gifts* sometimes.

Not in this case, obviously. No, this dog was supposed to teach Logan a lesson. This dog was punishment. Like confiscating the how-to-build-electronics books. Which was ridiculous, if you really thought about it, because now Logan was more determined than ever to build a lot of electronic things—not just weed whackers or remote controls, but a fire-breathing mechanical robot of such horrible destructive power that Robert would take one look at it and scream, "Oh my God, Logan! What have you done? It's eight hundred feet tall!" . . . and Logan would just laugh the way evil geniuses laughed ("Moo-hoo, ha, ha, ha!"), and Robert would flee the house in terror, never to return.

Maybe Logan should pretend that the dog was really a gift. He could act all wound up and excited about getting it. *A dog? No way! You mean it? Oh, boy! Gee, thanks, Robert!* Robert wouldn't be able to say anything because then he'd have to admit the "gift" was actually punishment. That would really tick him off.

Then again, a ticked-off Robert (more ticked off than usual, that is) could be dangerous.

"Don't you have anything to say?" Robert demanded.

Logan decided it was probably wisest to keep quiet. He shook his head and ate another spoonful of cereal.

Robert stood over him. "You know why we're getting you a dog, don't you?"

Sure, Logan answered silently. *You're hoping that getting me a dog will magically transform me into the next Devon Wallace.*

"I'm asking you a question," Robert stated in a clipped voice.

Logan shrugged.

"You know, this is exactly what I'm talking about," Robert said. "This attitude of yours. It needs a major adjustment."

"Sorry," Logan mumbled.

"Don't tell me you're sorry," Robert snapped. "You need to grow up. Training a dog will teach you the value of discipline and responsibility."

In spite of the fact that Robert's angry face was only inches from his own, Logan almost smiled. He couldn't believe that Robert had actually memorized what Mr. Wallace had said to him at the barbecue. Word for word. Maybe Logan had misjudged him. Maybe that phony-baloney interested act wasn't so phony-baloney after all.

"What's so funny?" Robert asked.

"Nothing," Logan said. He stood and carried his cereal bowl over to the sink.

"Rinse that bowl properly. I've noticed a lot of crud in the dishwasher lately. I don't want to have to replace it because you can't be bothered to rinse your dishes."

Logan ran the bowl under steaming hot water for several seconds. He held it up for Robert's inspection, then shoved it into the dishwasher with a *clink.*

Apparently it passed the test. Robert kept quiet.

"Where's Mom?" Logan asked.

"On the phone with the breeder," Robert said.

Logan's eyes narrowed. "The breeder?"

"We're getting Jack from the same place where the Wallaces got Otis. They specialize in purebred Labrador retrievers."

"Who's Jack?" Logan asked.

"The *dog*, Logan," Robert said with elaborate patience. "That's the dog's name."

Logan shook his head. The conversation wasn't making any sense. "Um . . . who says the dog's name is Jack?"

"I do," Robert said. "Jack was the name of my dog when I was growing up. It's a good name for a dog. A strong name."

"But what if it's a girl?"

Robert sighed. "It's *not* a girl because I told them we don't *want* a girl. I told them we want a male, about three months old, and chocolate brown. Like Otis."

"Oh, so that's what *we* want." Logan nodded slowly. "And—uh—this is *my* dog?"

Robert just gave him a look. "Don't make this a production, Logan."

Logan exhaled. *Okay.*

The way he saw it, it would be sort of like ordering an anchovy pizza for Robert—even though he knew Robert hated anchovies—then eating it himself because he loved anchovies. It would be pretty obvious that he'd ordered the pizza for himself all along. Not that it would do any good to point this out to Robert. He already seemed angry enough.

Robert marched out of the kitchen.

"So when are *we* getting the dog?" Logan called after him.

"Today." Robert's voice floated back from the front hall. "You and your mother are picking it up this morning. Now, if I've answered all your questions satisfactorily, maybe you'll excuse me. Some of us work for a living." He slammed the front door.

"See you later," Logan said to the empty kitchen.

Robert always went on about how he "worked for a living"—and worked very hard. Mom worked, too, though. She worked at the Newburg library, five days a week plus every other Saturday. But she never talked about how hard *she* worked.

Robert sold cars. Nice ones—mostly BMWs and Porsches, the kinds of cars that pretty much sold themselves. That didn't seem like very hard work to Logan. Then again, Robert liked to make a big deal about pretty much everything.

Logan looked sideways at his mother. She hadn't said a word since they'd left the house. They'd already been in the car for twenty minutes. Judging from the creases in her forehead, she wasn't in a good mood. Maybe she didn't want a dog, either.

Of course, Mom was a nervous driver. That might have something to do with her mood. The breeder lived in a hilly area west of Newburg, and the roads were twisty, with a lot of unexpected stoplights.

Mom didn't drive that much. Robert always insisted on doing the honors—since he was in the automotive business, as he liked to point out.

"So, Mom," Logan finally said. "Isn't buying a dog from a breeder pretty expensive?"

She nodded. Her grip tightened on the steering wheel.

"How much will Jack cost?" Logan asked.

"Six hundred dollars," she murmured.

"Six hundred dollars?" he cried. "You've got to be—"

"You should consider yourself lucky, Logan," she interrupted. "Until last night, Robert was going to spend that money on sending you to the Blue Mountain Camp for Boys. After Saturday he called and reserved a spot."

Logan shook his head. "Oh, okay," he said. "I get it. He decided a dog would be a better way to spend the money than boot camp. That way, even if I get into trouble again, *he'll* at least have the perfect pet. Right? Plus I'm sure the dog is cheaper."

Mom's lips thinned even more. "Logan, I don't know what to do with you," she said. "Robert may not be perfect—"

Understatement of the year, Logan thought.

"—but at least he's trying," Mom went on. "Why do you seem to do everything you possibly can to antagonize him?"

"Trying?" Logan burst out. "*Trying?* The only thing he's *trying* to do is turn me into Devon Wallace. Either that or get rid of me. And you just go along with everything he says!"

Logan's mother winced. "I try to defend you. I really do," she said quietly. "But with all the trouble you've had at school, and then the Wallaces' barbecue on top of that—" She shook her head. "You don't leave me a leg to stand on."

After that there really wasn't much to say. They rode in silence for a few moments.

"So we're really going to spend six hundred dollars on a dog," Logan said at last.

"We really are."

"That's totally insane," Logan said. "It's worse than insane. It's wrong."

"What do you mean, wrong?"

Logan searched for an argument. "I mean, there are dogs at dog pounds and animal shelters. And nobody wants them, and they don't cost a cent, and if people don't take them, they get put to sleep."

Logan's mother gave him a look out of the corner of her eye. "Since when do you care so much about homeless animals?"

"Whatever," Logan mumbled. "It just seems to me that if we're going to get a dog, we should get a dog from a shelter. That way Robert can spend the six hundred bucks on buying something nice for himself. Because that's what he really wants to do, anyway. And he should. Like he always tells me, it's *his* money."

Mom slowed to a stop at a red light. She turned to Logan. "Robert really wants this dog, Logan," she said. "This particular dog. A chocolate Lab."

"Exactly," Logan said. "That's *exactly* my point. Robert told me that we were getting this dog to teach me 'discipline and responsibility.' But that's not true. The truth is, Robert just wants a dog like Otis. Which is fine. He can get one. But if I'm going to spend all day with a dog for the next few months, trying to train it to pee outside and stuff, then I want to get one from a shelter. It's going to be a pain. I might as well feel good about myself. I might as well save a life."

Mom stared at him.

Logan took a deep breath. *Whew.* He wasn't really sure where that little speech had come from. He hardly ever said so much at one time. And yes, he *did* think that spending six hundred bucks on a dog was ridiculous and that rescuing a dog from the shelter was a noble thing to do. But deep down, he was mostly imagining the look on Robert's face when Robert came home tonight, expecting to see another Otis—and instead was greeted by the ugliest, stinkiest, mangiest mutt Logan could possibly find.

The light turned green. Mom stepped on the gas.

"So you're saying we should get two dogs," she said.

Logan shrugged. "I'm saying Robert should do whatever he wants for himself with the money. But he shouldn't try to make it seem like he's doing something for me. That's all."

Mom nodded.

All of a sudden, she pulled to the side of the road.

"What are you doing?" Logan asked.

"I'm turning around," she said. "Because you're right. If you're going to give this dog-training thing a real shot, then you should be able to do it with a dog you choose. We'll turn around and go back to town. I know where the shelter is."

"Really?" Logan asked. He was flabbergasted.

"Really," Mom said. She drew in a deep breath and fluttered her fingers on the steering wheel. Then she twisted in her seat so that she was facing Logan. "But if we get this dog, Logan, you have to promise me that you'll work hard every single day to train it. You have to promise me that you'll do things Robert's way for once."

Logan opened his mouth, then closed it.

He had no idea how to respond. The truth was, the very thought of doing things Robert's way turned his stomach. On the other hand, it *would* keep him out of boot camp. And maybe Logan could even train the dog to be some kind of genius, like Otis was supposed to be. Only, Logan wouldn't train the dog to fetch its own leash. No . . . he would train it to sneak into Robert's car dealership and pee on every single BMW Robert was trying to sell—and after that, to chew through every car seat in a frenzy of madness, all the while howling: *Ahh-ooo!*

Or not. But life was full of comprises. Even Robert could appreciate that.

Rudy Stagg's faxed response to
Sheila Davis's inquiry

June 22

Dear Miss Davis:

Thanks for your letter. I would have gotten back to you sooner, but I've been pretty busy.

About this dog bug: It is definitely real, and it is bad. I'm getting a lot of calls. People want me to come shoot their dogs before the dogs attack them.

The cases are all the same. I show up at somebody's house and the dog is lying somewhere, looking pretty much done for. At first I was waking the dogs up to see what happened, but every time it's the same thing: Faster than you can say your own name, the dog goes after whoever's closest. It could be me, it could be the owner, it could be the owner's kid.

So I don't even try to wake the dogs up anymore. I just walk in and shoot them, even if they aren't moving. Maybe that sounds harsh, but I've seen what happens when you don't act fast. Like the last case I had. It was at my friend John Bitterman's house. He had two female sheepdogs, Morgan and Oakley. They were both dead by the time I got there.

There was blood everywhere. Bitterman had a huge gash behind his left knee where he'd been mauled. He told me what happened.

Both dogs had been sick for a while—the same

symptoms as all the other dogs. Bitterman thought it might be rabies. But Morgan and Oakley had been vaccinated. So that was out. He took them to his vet, but the vet couldn't figure out what was wrong.

Then they stopped eating and started sleeping all the time. That was when he gave me a call.

The very same day, before I got there, Morgan attacked Oakley. The dogs had never so much as growled at each other. They were littermates, peas in a pod. But Morgan chewed off half of Oakley's tail before suddenly dropping dead. And Oakley didn't move an inch while Morgan was doing it. That was the creepy part. She didn't even open her eyes.

Bitterman figured she had to be dead, too, until a couple of minutes later, when she snapped out of it and chased him through the house, howling. He said her tail was a dripping, bloody stump. He managed to get into the upstairs bathroom and slam the door in her face, but not before Oakley bit the back of his leg. She threw her body against the door over and over. Bitterman said probably thirty times in all. After that, she died.

What I'm trying to say here is, if you want a story, you've got it. I'm happy to help you. The cops sure don't seem to know what they're doing.

Sincerely,
Rudy Stagg

CHAPTER FIVE

"Well, that's all the dogs we have, sweetheart. They're all such darlings, I'm sure it's hard to choose. Would you like to take another look?"

Logan shrugged.

Coming to the shelter wasn't turning out to be such a great idea. For one thing, it reeked. There were rows and rows of cages—probably thirty in all—and the dogs didn't just live in them; they went to the bathroom inside them, too. (Quite a bit, it seemed.) The dogs wouldn't shut up, either. Logan had never heard more barking, yowling, and whining in his entire life. The actual shelter part of the building didn't have any windows, so the racket and the stink got trapped inside. The whole place was lit by buzzing fluorescent tubes, the kind that made everybody look as if they hadn't slept in years.

But the worst part of all was this woman—Ms. Dougherty, the one who was in charge. She was a chubby, annoying, all-smiles type who insisted on calling everybody "sweetheart" and who talked to the caged-up animals in one of those idiotic baby voices: *"Oh, yesh. You're shuch a precioush li'l baby girl. Yesh, you are."* Whenever she opened her mouth, Logan felt like barfing.

He glanced at the cages again. "You really don't have any other dogs?" he asked. All the dogs here were too . . . well, for lack of a better word, *cute.* Most of them were puppies, all fuzzy and cuddly.

Weren't animal shelters supposed to house the dregs of doggy society? The ugliest of the ugly? The exact opposite of Otis?

Ms. Dougherty looked surprised. "No. I'm afraid we—"

A sudden commotion erupted behind the double doors at the far end of the room. Logan could hear shouting, mixed with a high-pitched bark. A moment later the doors burst open and a stocky man barreled out, clutching his arm. "Get that needle into her before she bites one of you, too," he called over his shoulder. He glanced at Ms. Dougherty and shook his head. "I don't think this one is worth saving, Ruth."

"Do you have a dog back there?" Logan asked. "Another dog?"

Ms. Dougherty's smile had vanished. "Well, yes," she admitted. "The dogcatchers found a wild dog out on Route Seventy-eight, in the Cascades. She's in the examination room. But the problem is that—"

"A wild dog?" Logan interrupted. His hopes rose.

"That's right," Ms. Dougherty said. The smile returned, a shade wider and more sugary than before. "And that's the problem, sweetheart. She's a *wild animal*. Ed's the third person she's bitten since she was brought in. I wouldn't recommend her as a pet."

"Can't I take a look at her?"

Ms. Dougherty hesitated. "Well, I—I guess it wouldn't do any harm to take a look," she mumbled with an awkward, squeaky little laugh. "Why not? Come this way."

She turned and walked toward the double doors. Her shoes clattered on the tile floor. Logan and his mother followed her into what looked like a big hospital emergency room. It was sterile and white, lined with shelves full of pill bottles. There was an electronic scale, an IV unit, and other sorts of medical machinery. It smelled sort of like a dentist's office.

In the center of the room was a metal table. A skinny reddish dog lay on it, flanked by two guys. They were wearing white lab coats, but they clearly weren't vets—they looked like teenagers. One of them held a hypodermic syringe in his hand. It was empty, as if he'd just injected whatever it held into the dog.

Logan stepped forward and peered at the dog.

She looked half dead. She was almost as big as Otis—but much, much thinner. Her coat was filthy and matted. Logan could see the outline of her ribs. Her tongue lolled from her mouth. Her eyes were wide and glassy. One of her legs was bleeding.

"Here she is," Ms. Dougherty said.

Logan glanced back at her. *And?* He was waiting for Ms. Dougherty to walk up to the dog and start talking to her: *"Hel-looo, li'l ba-beee, yesh, yesh."* But Ms. Dougherty stuck close to the door and didn't say another word.

"Her rabies test came back," the guy with the syringe said. "It was negative."

A look of relief flashed across Ms. Dougherty's face. "Let Ed and the others know immediately."

Still, she didn't go up and start cooing over the dog.

"How old is she?" Logan asked.

"About ten months," the other guy said. "She may not look so good, but she's actually pretty healthy. More than you can say for a lot of the strays we've found recently. There's a disease going around, you know. But this one doesn't have it."

"So how long will it be before she can go home with someone?" Logan asked. He couldn't take his eyes off the dog. She was just so . . . *ugly.* So not Otis.

"I really don't know about this, Logan," Mom whispered.

All of a sudden, the dog started to squirm. The two guys grabbed her. She ran in place, almost like a cartoon animal—her paws scratching the slick surface of the metal with a sputtering *click-click-click*. She barked at Logan.

"This one just doesn't go under," the guy with the syringe said. "We gave her enough tranquilizer for—"

The dog barked again, this time so loudly that Logan flinched. She wouldn't stop wriggling. A moment later, she twisted free of the guys and jumped off the table, scrambling straight for Logan.

His body tensed. But the dog stopped in front of him and gazed at him. Her eyes never wavered for an instant. They were locked on Logan. She wasn't wagging her tail or panting in his face, the way Otis always did. She was just standing there.

Slowly, her paws slid out from under her, until she was splayed on the concrete floor. And still she stared up at Logan. She almost looked as if she were trying to tell him something. *Please get me out of here. Please. I can't stand another second with Ms. Dougherty.*

Cautiously, he bent down and touched the dog's head. She looked at him for a moment longer. Then she closed her eyes.

The guys in the white coats exchanged puzzled glances.

"What's the matter?" Mom asked.

"Well, actually, I was worried she was going to bite the kid," the guy with the syringe said. "She's never let anyone touch her without a fight." He shook his head. "It must be the tranquilizer."

"Maybe she likes me," Logan said.

Nobody answered.

Logan smiled.

"What is it?" Mom asked.

"Nothing." Logan glanced up at Ms. Dougherty. "So. How long before we can take her home?"

Ms. Dougherty blinked. "You want this dog?"

"Logan, please," Mom said. "This isn't a good idea at all. She's completely wild. We should go to the breeder, okay? Coming here was a bad idea. I'm sorry. It was my fault."

"But this dog needs help," Logan said. "And I'm willing to help her. Robert wants to teach me the value of discipline, right? What better way to learn discipline than to tame a wild dog? Besides, if there was ever a dog that needed rescuing, she's it."

Mom sighed.

"Well, you'll have to wait until she's had all her shots," Ms. Dougherty said. "And you'll have to fill out some paperwork, too, of course. Just some forms and waivers and things like that, so we can be sure that you're serious about owning a dog."

"I'm serious," Logan said.

"Logan," Mom said. "Please."

"I am," Logan insisted. "She'll be *my* dog. I'll take responsibility for her. I'll buy all the food and her leash and water dish and everything. And if you're worried about Robert, I'll tell you what. I'll throw him a bone. I'll name her Jack in his honor."

Mom frowned. "It's a girl dog, Logan," she said.

"I know. But look at it this way. Robert wanted a dog named Jack. Now he'll have one. So we'll all be happy, right?"

Mom didn't answer. She just gave a weary sigh.

"Everybody has to make compromises sometimes," Logan murmured, mostly to himself. He glanced down at the dog. "Right, Jack?"

RECENT DOG ATTACKS LINKED TO UNKNOWN DISEASE

BY SHEILA DAVIS

REDMONT, OR, June 24—The peculiar rise in the number of local dog attacks can be traced to an unidentified disease, according to Sheriff John Van Wyck of the Redmont Sheriff's Office.

In the past three weeks six dog attacks have been reported, more than twice the number of all such attacks reported in the area in the last ten years. Local animal health officials are baffled. Veterinarian Claudia Juarez described a typical course of symptoms: At first, the dogs wheeze and foam at the mouth. They develop balance problems and often trip or fall down. After this first stage, they sleep more than usual. The end stage of the disease is marked by intense and continuous aggression, with dogs attacking any living creatures indiscriminately. Eventually the diseased animals die, "basically of exhaustion," said Dr. Juarez. "As far as I can tell, their systems overload with so much adrenaline that sooner or later their hearts can't take the strain anymore."

Rudy Stagg, a home security consultant and dog trainer based in Redmont, has begun to develop a reputation as an unofficial dog vigilante, a role that was thrust upon him because he trained two of the dogs involved in the first attacks. "I wasn't a dog killer before, but that's pretty much what I've become," he said.

Stagg warned that any sick dog has the potential to be extremely dangerous. "Even if they look like they're sleeping, they could attack at any time," he said.

Sheriff Van Wyck has contacted the Research Center for Infectious Diseases at Portland University and asked for their help in identifying the disease and curing it. "I'm confident the situation will be brought under control in a matter of days," he said. "In the meantime, watch your pets carefully. If they slobber more than usual or seem listless in any way, please contact the sheriff's office or your local vet immediately. These cases should be handled by the proper authorities."

CHAPTER
SIX

The phone was ringing. Westerly could hear the bothersome jangle from the dirt driveway. He shook his head. He wasn't going to let a phone call disturb the final moments of his walk with Jasmine. This was their favorite time of the week: the Wednesday afternoon hike into town for food and mail. It was five miles each way, half on roads, half on mountain trails. Four hours total of fresh mountain air and sunshine. Or rain. But not today.

Jasmine loved it. She loved visiting Joe Bixby's general store. Her tail would start wagging about a hundred yards away because she could smell Sam—Joe Bixby's big, rangy, blue-eyed Siberian husky. The second she burst through the door, she and Sam would start jumping on each other and barking. They would scurry around the aisles and chase each other while Westerly loaded up his backpack. And when they were too tired to keep playing, Joe Bixby would give them each a little treat: a piece of salami, a hunk of cheese. It was always enough to perk Jasmine up for the walk home.

That Wednesday afternoon hike to town was pretty much the only time Westerly enjoyed dealing with other human beings. Or *one* human being, anyway. Joe was a decent sort. Like most of the people in town, he was scruffy and rugged. He understood that Westerly preferred to be left alone. He wasn't much of a talker himself.

"So," Westerly said to Jasmine. He grunted a little under the weight of the backpack as he walked around the side of the house. "Who do you think could be calling me?"

Jasmine growled, then ran up the porch steps. She stumbled a little at the top. She nearly lost her balance, her eyes darting between Westerly and the screen door.

Westerly grinned at her. She wasn't a huge fan of the phone, either.

"Don't worry about it, Jazz," he said. He trudged up behind her, slinging the pack off his shoulder and unlocking the door. "We'll let the machine pick up."

Truth be told, he would have let the machine pick up no matter what. He always screened his calls. Usually it was just a salesperson wanting Westerly to subscribe to *Time* or to buy a cell phone or some other nonsense. People who knew Westerly knew better than to call him. E-mails or letters were the best ways to communicate.

The machine clicked.

Westerly stood next to Jasmine and rubbed the back of her neck, staring at the little black box beside the phone.

"You've reached Dr. Craig Westerly," the machine announced. "Leave a message."

There was a beep.

"Craig, it's Harold. If you're there, pick up."

Harold?

Westerly's stomach dropped. Harold would never, ever call him. Not unless—

He darted forward and picked up the phone.

"Hello? I'm here. Harold?"

"Craig," Harold replied. His voice sounded strangely high-pitched. He exhaled. "We've got a problem."

Westerly stared out the window at the evergreen tree. "What's up?"

"We need your paper on prion diseases," Harold said. "The situation here has changed."

"Didn't you get my e-mail?" Westerly asked. He drummed his fingers on his jeans. "I couldn't find it. I looked all over." He really *had* searched high and low for the paper. But after a couple of hours of rummaging through dusty old boxes and file cabinets, he remembered that he'd tossed it out years ago. The only papers he'd kept were those having to do with his *new* research—like inventing an inhalable flu vaccine.

"Yes, I received your e-mail," Harold said. "I just assumed you didn't want to be bothered. I figured you were still angry."

Why would I be angry? Westerly wanted to say. *Oh, right. Because you fired me seven years ago just for spite.*

"Craig?" Harold asked.

"If I had found it, I would have sent it to you," Westerly said.

"You always wanted to be a respected scientist, didn't you?" Harold asked.

Westerly frowned into the phone. "What's that supposed to mean?"

"I'm offering you a chance to make that happen," Harold said. "I'm offering you a chance to come back to the university."

"Excuse me?" Westerly couldn't quite grasp what he was hearing.

"That's right. It's your choice. I'm giving you the opportunity to join us again."

Westerly opened his mouth. Then he closed it. His throat was dry. Never in his wildest daydreams would he have imagined *this:* that Harold would call to invite him back to work. It could only mean one thing. Harold was in some kind of trouble. He'd actually swallowed his pride and stooped to call Westerly—the guy who couldn't get along with anyone, the "mad scientist of the mountains." (Harold had once called him that in an e-mail a few years back.) The situation was *that* bad.

"The disease is spreading," Harold added, as if answering an unspoken question. "I've had to order the equipment to run full-scale tests for the presence of prions. All the evidence so far seems to indicate that it's a strain we've never seen before. It's stronger and faster. The incubation period is much shorter. Three weeks from infection until death. The evidence also seems to indicate that it can be transmitted through dog bites. . . ."

As Harold continued, Westerly found he could no longer listen. He could only stare at Jasmine. She'd stumbled on the stairs just now.

Stumbling was one of the first symptoms of a prion disease.

Westerly would have thought nothing of the stumble if Harold hadn't called. None of this had crossed his mind in three days—not since he'd looked around for the paper. Not once. This was a gift Westerly had and one that served him well in his work: If certain thoughts interfered with his ability to focus, he simply stowed them somewhere, in some hidden part of his brain, and forgot about them until the appropriate time. Some people called it compartmentalizing. Others—his ex-wife, for instance—said that *compartmentalizing* was just a fancy way of dressing up the truth, which was that Westerly was self-absorbed and rude and thoughtless. . . .

". . . Are you still there?"

Westerly nodded. "Yes. Yes, I'm sorry."

"So what's your answer?" Harold asked.

"You'll have to excuse me, Harold," Westerly mumbled, wrenching his attention away from Jasmine. "I didn't hear the question."

It was just a stumble, he told himself. *Don't read into it.*

"For God's sake!" Harold snapped. "Can't you listen to me for five minutes? Do you still hate me that much?"

Hate you?

Well, *hate* was a strong word . . . although, yes, Westerly disliked him. But that hardly mattered. This was a crisis. Yet Harold had to turn it into something personal. He had to bring up all the old issues again—issues of not getting along with people, issues that had nothing to do with the matter at hand. In short, Harold had to place himself and his problems over the seriousness of this disease.

It was politics. Stupid politics.

Westerly's lips pressed into a tight line. So. Nothing had changed at all in seven years. Not one thing. And in that instant, all the sour memories of the university came flooding back, washing away any temptation he might have had to take Harold up on his offer. There was no way he would go back there. He'd help Harold as much as he could from home, but that was it. End of story. Besides, if the disease was spreading, then a trip to Portland would endanger Jasmine's life. And that was a risk he refused to take.

"I need an answer, Craig," Harold said.

"I'll tell you what you need to know over the phone," Westerly said. "From day one, my theory has always been that to cure prion disease, you need to synthesize an antidote from an immune animal. Get your hands on an immune dog, and I'll talk you through the process—"

"That's part of the problem," Harold interrupted. "We can't find an immune dog. All the dogs at the university are already sick." His voice rose. "This is an emergency!"

"You can't be serious," Westerly said.

"Dead serious," Harold said.

Westerly couldn't answer. He couldn't even breathe. The cabin spun around him like water circling a drain, faster and faster.

It's happening, he thought. *It's really happening, just the way I said it would.*

He'd been right all along. But that didn't make him feel any better.

"I hope you know that I'm telling you all this in the strictest of confidence," Harold added. "We haven't made this information public because we don't want to start a panic. I'm telling you now because I want you to understand how bad the situation is. So you have a choice to make. Either you start behaving like a responsible scientist, or you keep hiding out there in the woods."

Click.

"Harold?" Westerly croaked. "Harold?"

But the line was dead.

The she-pup had never known contentment until the day she was let out of the shelter. She'd known happiness at different points in her young life: in the forest, before the sickness had wiped out her pack . . . but this was different. To feel the sun on her coat, to have a full belly, to breathe the scent of the evergreens, to be free—that was what it meant to be alive.

The boy had rescued her.

She'd been too dazed to show him gratitude at first. She simply slept as he whisked her off to her new home. But now, at the moment of arrival, she knew she had come to a place where things made sense. Here, she had a companion.

The boy kept close to her side. He protected her. There was a connection between them.

The memory of the wild—of Mother and White Paws and the slow death of her pack . . . all of it began to fade. She was part of a new pack now. A pack of two. The boy had restored order. He had given her safety. He had given her a name.

She was no longer a starving puppy in the forest, fighting for survival.

She was Jack.

CHAPTER SEVEN

Logan's first order of business was to train Jack to pee and poop outside.

He already had a specific place in mind: the little grassy area in the backyard, right under Robert's hammock. Jack seemed to want to go there, too. She kept tugging on her leather leash, trying to drag Logan toward that exact spot.

So far, so good.

From what Logan could tell, training a dog to pee and poop someplace—or to do anything, really—wasn't all that hard. You just had to be patient. You had to do the same thing again and again, in the exact same place. You had to approach it from a scientific point of view. No cute talk or games or face licking or any of that. Nope. Strictly science.

Over the past three days (the time it had taken for the shelter to make sure Jack wasn't sick), Logan had buried himself in a bunch of books on dog training. He was going to become an expert. Of course, part of the reason he read so much was to keep Robert off his back. Robert had thrown a major fit about Jack, even worse than Logan had expected. *What do you mean, you didn't go to the breeder? I had a deposit there! I don't want the money back! I want a purebred! How could you let Logan sucker you into this!*" . . . blah, blah, blah.

After the freak-out, though, Robert had kept to himself.

Especially when he saw Logan reading. Maybe he really *did* think Logan was trying to shape up.

More likely, though, he was just saving up for another explosion. Whatever.

As it turned out, Logan could have read a lot less because most of the training books said pretty much the same thing. He kind of felt ripped off. The books all had lame titles—*I Just Bought a Puppy! So What Do I Do Now?*—and all the covers featured glossy photos of big-haired women with fake-looking dogs. The books were written in stupid, flowery language, too, like romance novels or something. *"Dear dog owner, The most important gift you can give your new mate is your heart. . . ."* Blecch. Logan heard Ms. Dougherty's voice in his head whenever he cracked one open. And they could all be summed up in six words:

1. Reward good behavior.
2. Ignore bad behavior.

That was it.

Interestingly, *punishing* a dog for bad behavior was the wrong way to go. Punishment only made a dog sullen or withdrawn—or in the worst cases, violent. (Sort of like people, if you really thought about it. Robert could learn a thing or two from these books.)

Sure, there were a couple of tricks. One was to get the dog to associate good behavior with a treat, like a doggy biscuit or a piece of bacon. That way the dog would *want* to be good. And if you threw in a pleasing noise of some sort—like a bell or a click or a whistle—then that was even better because dogs responded well to "sonic cues." Along those lines, it was best to use simple, one- or two-word commands. *"Sit." "Down." "Heel." "Play dead."*

There was really nothing more to it than that. Say the command; give a treat; ring a bell; bingo. Pretty soon the dog would do whatever you wanted. You wouldn't even have to use the treats for very long because soon hearing the "sonic cue" after the command would be rewarding enough. According to the books, anyway.

Logan made sure all the bases were covered. For treats, he'd swiped the bacon bits from Mom's spice cabinet. For the noise part, he'd built a special device: the Logan Moore Sonic Cue Gun, or LMSCG. He'd taken the bicycle bell from Mom's old three-speed and fastened it on top of a water gun, then rigged the trigger with a bit of fishing wire so that when he pulled it, the wire yanked on the bell's ringer. All he had to do was aim the thing at Jack. Point, squeeze, *brrring!* It was pretty loud, too.

"All right, Jack," Logan said. "Time to do your business."

Jack stopped tugging at her leash. She sniffed the lawn.

Logan tried to yank her over to the hammock. She seemed to have changed her mind about wanting to go there. And for such a scrawny dog, she was actually pretty strong. Logan had to shove the LMSCG into his pocket and use both hands to pull her.

"Come on, Jack," Logan grunted. "Come on. Right over here."

She started tearing at the grass with her front paws.

Uh-oh. The hammock was close to the kitchen window. Mom and Robert were in there right now. The screen was shut, but the window was open. If Robert saw Jack ripping up the lawn . . . well, Logan would just try to keep quiet. Anyway, he was supposed to ignore bad behavior. Digging a hole in the backyard certainly fell into that category.

Logan chewed his lip. He could hear Robert and Mom at the table.

". . . can't believe we let him bring that mutt home," Robert was muttering. He sounded disgusted. "This is *your* fault. This has disaster written all over it."

"But I think it's good for Logan," Mom said. "He feels that he made his own decision, you know? He's taking responsibility for it. It's not like we're forcing something on him again. I mean, you saw all those books he has on dog training. And besides, he does have a point about the money. You can still get a purebred Lab if you really want one—"

"This house isn't big enough for two dogs," Robert snapped. "And you know it. And what if Jack has this disease everybody's talking about? What if she's sick?"

Mom sighed. "She's not sick, Robert. She was examined thoroughly. Look, just be patient, okay? Let's make the best of this."

Logan stared down at Jack.

Come on, come on, he urged silently. *Stop digging. Stop it. . . .*

Suddenly Jack lifted her head and lowered her rear end. She peed, staring into space. She wasn't right under the hammock, but she was close enough.

"Good girl!" Logan exclaimed.

He reached into his front pocket for a handful of bacon bits. As Jack gobbled them up, Logan pulled the LMSCG from his back pocket. He had to struggle to hold on to the leash at the same time. It was all a little awkward. But he managed to get off a ring before she'd finished the treats. Jack wagged her scraggly tail and raised her eyes, as if to say, *No more bacon bits?*

Logan grinned. "Okay, Jack," he said. "Next time I'll—"

"Logan! What are you doing out there?"

Robert's nose was mashed against the window screen.

"I . . ." Logan didn't know what to say.

"Did you just let the dog pee on my lawn?" Robert demanded.

("*My* lawn." Not "*our* lawn." Not "*the* lawn." *Robert's lawn.*) "Well, yeah," Logan said. "I just figured it would be better if she peed out here than—"

"Take her on the *sidewalk*, Logan!" Robert shouted. "It's bad for the grass! Get her out of the backyard! Now!"

Jack's tail stopped wagging. She barked at the window.

Logan turned away and pulled at the leash. But Jack didn't seem to want to move.

"What's that bell you got there?" Robert asked.

"It's supposed to help with the training," Logan said.

"Why do you need it? The Wallaces don't use a bell with Otis."

"I was just following the advice of the books," Logan said.

"What are you, an expert on dog training now?" Robert demanded.

Why are you still talking to me if you want me to get Jack out of the backyard? Logan wondered. But instead of asking the question out loud, he bent down and picked Jack up, cradling her like a big baby, and carried her away from the window as fast as possible. In a situation like this, it was best just to get her out of Robert's sight.

Not that Logan was going to stop training her to pee under the hammock. He was just going to wait until Robert went back to the car dealership.

Weirdly enough, the hardest part of owning Jack turned out to be finding a toy that she liked.

You couldn't just *give* her a toy, Logan realized. If you tried, she would sniff at it, then just stare at you as if to say, *Come on, man. This is a fuzzy bumblebee. Don't insult me. Give me the good stuff.*

It was actually pretty funny. The day after she arrived, Logan took her to the pet store to load up on plastic bones and rawhide sticks and squeaky stuffed animals. She seemed pretty interested in the stuff while he was picking it out. Especially the bumblebee. She even barked at it. He spent nearly thirty bucks—just about every penny he had. But when he got home and dumped the loot in the middle of his room, she didn't even bother to *look* at it.

Instead she headed straight for his closet and clamped her jaws around his baseball mitt.

"No, no, Jack," Logan whispered. "Drop it."

He bit his lip to keep from laughing. He didn't want to raise his voice. If Robert overheard him ordering her to drop the baseball mitt (the baseball mitt that *Robert* had wasted *Robert's* hard-earned money on, and why didn't Logan play baseball, anyway—didn't he know it was the greatest sport ever invented?) . . . well, in a nutshell, that wouldn't be good.

Jack started shaking her head. She bared her teeth, swinging the mitt wildly from side to side—as if the baseball mitt were really just another meal.

"Come on, Jack," Logan whispered. "Drop it."

She swung the mitt harder.

Logan darted forward and snatched the mitt from her jaws.

"Play with your toys," he commanded, holding the mitt high over his head. "Go on. They're all right there for you."

But Jack sat still on her haunches, staring at the mitt. A low growl rumbled deep in her throat. Maybe the dogs in those books were dumb, but Jack wasn't. She knew exactly what she wanted.

"Come on, girl," Logan pleaded. "This isn't a toy. Your toys are right behind you. They're all brand-new."

Jack's growl grew louder. Her eyes flashed to Logan, as if to say, *So what if they're new? That's the lamest pile of crap I've ever seen in my life.*

Logan grinned. He shot an anxious glance toward the door. In a way, he could relate to Jack's frustration. After all, he always hated it when Robert tried to give *him* stuff that he didn't want. Like the baseball mitt. Or the model airplane set. Perfect example. *Robert* was the one who thought model airplanes were so cool. He'd bought it so *he* could use it. But after a while, he'd gotten bored with it (the way he always did), so it had been sitting in Logan's closet for months, collecting dust—until Logan had decided to build the LMMRC.

The thing was, Logan had never even *thought* of it as a model airplane set. He didn't see it that way. He saw a box full of raw parts, the beginnings of a master remote control. So if Jack didn't see a dumb baseball mitt, but instead saw something else—a leather chew toy, the head of her worst enemy, a magical being that could spring to life at any time and kill everybody in the house when they least expected it . . . well, who was Logan to take that away from her just because of what people said a baseball mitt was *supposed* to be?

"You know what, girl?" Logan whispered. "I'm sorry. Here you go."

He handed the mitt back to Jack.

She snatched it in her jaws and started swinging it again—even more crazily than before. It flew across the room and smacked against the door. She barked at the sound.

Uh-oh. Logan swallowed.

"Logan?" Robert called from downstairs. "What's going on in there? That dog isn't breaking anything, is she?"

"Uh, no," Logan said. "She's just playing."

Jack pounced on the mitt and started banging it against the wall: *thump-thump-thump*.

"Stop it, Jack," Logan begged, even though he was laughing. He grabbed the mitt again and tossed it on his bed. She scrambled after it.

"Logan!" Robert called.

"Uh . . . um . . . don't worry," Logan shouted back. He ran to the door and locked it, then hurried over to the bed and flicked on the clock radio on his nightstand. The tinny, static-blurred voice of a female news reporter filled the room.

Good, Logan thought. That should drown out Jack's shenanigans.

". . . and still, nobody can seem to determine the cause of the disease," the reporter was saying. "So far, over thirty dogs in Redmont have died."

Logan's ears perked up.

"We're fortunate to have with us here today Mr. Rudy Stagg, a part-time dog trainer based in Redmont, who's had lots of first-hand experience with the disease," the woman continued. "Thanks for joining us, Mr. Stagg."

"My pleasure," a gruff-sounding man answered.

"So what's your take on all this?" the woman asked. "What advice would you give the dog owners of southern Oregon?"

Logan stared at the radio. He'd heard this reporter before. He couldn't remember her name. But usually she sounded ditzy and lighthearted. Not today. Today she sounded downright depressed. Either that or angry.

"I would tell them to keep an eye on their pets," Mr. Stagg said. "And if they start acting funny—shaking, foaming at the mouth, that kind of thing—don't get near them. Call me immediately. My number is—"

"Don't you think it would be a better idea for people to call the CDC?" the woman interrupted.

"The what, now?"

"The Centers for Disease Control and Prevention," the woman said. "They're sending a team of specialists here to investigate the problem."

"Well, if you ask me, that's about the worst idea I've heard all year," Stagg drawled. "Once the government gets involved, you lose all control. They come in here with their fancy thugs and their black helicopters and the next thing you know, you're living in a police state. Call me or do it yourself, but—"

Logan flipped the dial to a heavy metal station.

He hated listening to angry-sounding people. He heard enough of that just walking around his own house every day. But still, he couldn't help feeling nervous. *The CDC is coming to investigate the problem.* That sounded pretty serious.

Forget it. Logan shook his head. He shouldn't worry about it. Whatever the "problem" was, it wasn't *his* problem. Jack was fine. The shelter guys had promised Logan that she was perfectly healthy.

He glanced at her.

She'd gotten back into his closet. Now she was chewing contentedly on one of the loafers that Mom and Robert had bought him for formal occasions.

Logan smiled. *Good girl,* he thought. He'd always hated those shoes.

AN OPEN LETTER TO THE DOG
OWNERS OF REDMONT:
PROTECT YOURSELF
AND YOUR PETS!
DON'T BE BULLIED BY THE CDC!

Dear Dog Owners,

My name is Rudy Stagg. Many of you already know me. I have been a home security consultant and dog trainer in Redmont for the past twenty years. I have an impeccable reputation.

You may have heard public service announcements on the radio recently, telling you to contact the police or the Centers for Disease Control and Prevention if your dog appears listless or ill. Everyone knows this is because of the strange disease that's been killing our dogs.

But here's what you may not know: The CDC is an arm of the federal government. Once you hand your dog over to them, they will take it to a "quarantine center" and you will never see your pet again. What's more, the CDC will require you to *move out of your house* for forty-eight hours while agents "decontaminate" it. And if you have other pets, they will take those animals, too.

Who knows what these people are *really* doing

with our pets? Who knows what they're *really* doing in our houses?

You are not obligated to hand over your dog to a stranger just because that stranger claims to have authority.

Don't let them scare you. Allow your dog to die with dignity—and stand up for your right to live your life free of government interference. I am setting up a training program to instruct people on how to shoot their dogs in the most painless way possible. Lessons start at $45.00 an hour.

To contact me for lessons or dog training, please call (503) 555-8764 or e-mail me at rudy@rudystagg.com.

CHAPTER EIGHT

In less than a week, Jack started getting the hang of peeing and pooping outside the house. Logan couldn't believe it. Sure, she still slipped up every so often (she actually seemed to enjoy going on the floor in Mom and Robert's bathroom, which was sort of comical)—but at the end of day five, it was official: She'd only had one accident.

The bacon bit–LMSCG combo was really paying off. Maybe *he* should write a book about training dogs. It was weird; he felt more proud of himself than he had in a long time—as if he'd just invented the coolest machine ever, like an ultrapowerful miniaturizing ray that would shrink Robert down to the size of a plastic soldier so Logan could flush him down the toilet.

And all he'd done was housebreak a wild mutt. Or come close, anyway. He probably could have trained her completely, too, if Robert hadn't been around.

Robert just didn't understand the "ignore bad behavior" part of dog training. Whenever he came home from work, he would follow Logan and Jack from room to room, waiting for Jack to mess up. It was the same old script every single night. The house was starting to feel like the set of a bad TV show.

Robert: That dog better not be going into my bathroom.
Logan: If she does, just ignore her.

Robert: Ignore her? That's easy for you to say. It's not *your* bathroom.

Logan: Yeah, but I'm the one who has to clean it up.

Robert: Look! There she goes! I knew it! Bad girl! Bad!

Logan: Shhh. All you have to do is pick her up and take her outside.

Robert: While she's taking a leak? Are you out of your mind? Bad girl!

Logan: If you keep talking to her like that, she's going to develop a neurotic habit and pee in here even more. If you want her to stop, pick her up and take her outside—

Robert: Bad girl! No! Bad! Do something, Logan! Do something!

The funniest part (or unfunniest, depending on how you looked at it) was that Jack would usually start barking at Robert at this point. Sometimes Jack would bark so viciously that Robert would get a little nervous. Then Robert would start in on Logan again, and Jack would just bark even more loudly. And all the stupidity would have been so easy to avoid—that is, if Robert had bothered trying to learn anything about dogs.

The only reason Jack barked at Robert was to *protect* Logan. Jack thought of Logan as her master. The pack leader. So if Robert yelled at Logan, he was threatening the whole pack order. Logan wasn't just making this stuff up. He'd read it in all those books. He was the one who spent the most time with her; he was the one who disciplined her; he was the one who fed and rewarded her—so *obviously* she would think of him as her master.

Of course, it would never occur to Robert that any creature could possibly consider Logan a master. *Robert* was the master. The All-Knowing Dictator of Everything. Period, infinity, until the end of time.

*   *   *

"We have to get rid of that dog," Robert said one morning.

Logan stopped chewing. He glanced down at Jack. She was sitting beside his chair, looking up at him with her bright eyes. Then he turned to Mom, who was concentrating very hard on buttering her toast. He put down his spoon and swallowed, his thoughts racing. Was this something about that dog disease?

"Why?" he asked finally.

"Because you aren't training her right," Robert said. He glowered at Logan across the kitchen table. "I found bite marks in my tennis racket. Now I'm going to have to get a new one. You know how much a brand-new tennis racket costs?"

Logan stared back at him, feeling a weird rush of both anger and relief. So this *wasn't* about the dog disease. He pushed aside his bowl. "Where did you leave the tennis racket?" he asked.

"What does that have to do with anything?" Robert asked.

"You just have to be careful, that's all," Logan said. "If you leave things lying around, Jack will probably find them and chew on them. All puppies chew on things."

"Otis doesn't," Robert said.

Logan shot another quick glance at Mom. She was still hiding behind her toast. Typical. Well, maybe Logan would apply some of his dog-training techniques with Robert. He could ignore the guy. If he ignored Robert's stupid behavior, maybe Robert would stop acting like an idiot all the time. Anything was worth a shot.

"Otis isn't a puppy," Logan said. He stood and rinsed his cereal bowl. "Jack's still less than a year old. I've gotten her some chew toys, but she doesn't really like them."

"So how come she doesn't ruin *your* stuff?" Robert asked.

"She does," Mom said. "Jack chewed up Logan's nice shoes."

Logan turned to Jack. She was still eyeing everyone's food. *Can you believe that?* he asked Jack silently. *Mom actually stuck up for me! Somebody should call that woman news reporter, pronto, because this is a great moment in history, far more important than any dumb disease; it is a milestone, and will probably never be repeated in our lifetimes.*

"Logan hates formal occasions," Robert said. "He probably gave Jack those shoes on purpose so she could ruin them."

Mom didn't answer. Today, for whatever reason, she appeared to be fed up with Robert's stupidity as well.

"Why is she so bad?" Robert demanded. "Huh, Logan? Why?"

"Because she's a puppy," Logan said. "She's only been with us six days. Not even. Six days this afternoon. She's bound to misbehave every now and then."

All of a sudden Jack hopped up on Logan's chair and started sniffing the table.

"No!" Robert shouted. His face turned red. "No! Get off! Bad girl! No—"

"Down," Logan commanded. His tone was calm and firm.

Jack turned at the sound of his voice. She jumped off the chair and trotted over to him.

"Good girl," Logan said. He patted her head and pulled the LMSCG from his back pocket. With his free hand he fished a few bacon bits from his front pocket and fed them to her. He squeezed the trigger as she licked his fingers: *Brrriiing!*

Robert shook his head. "This is exactly what I'm talking about," he said. "The jumping up on chairs, the—"

"What?" Mom cried. She slammed down her butter knife with a clatter. "Logan got the dog to *stop* jumping on the chair! Isn't that what you wanted? What's your problem, Robert? *I* think Logan's doing a good job with the dog. And I'd appreciate it if you started leaving him alone."

Robert and Logan both gaped at her for a moment.

"My property is being destroyed," Robert said stiffly.

Jack barked at him.

"Your tennis racket is *our* property," Mom said. "We're a family, remember? We share things."

"You might want to remind your son of that," Robert snapped.

Logan stared at them. He started to feel weirdly detached, as if he were watching the scene unfold on cheap, grainy videotape. This was possibly the dumbest argument in the history of planet Earth. But somehow it was so *serious.* Mom and Robert were glaring at each other. Any satisfaction that Logan felt over Mom's decision to side with him began to melt away like the butter that was sitting in the sun on the kitchen table. Why was Robert so mad, anyway? This was stupid even for *him.*

"Robert, listen," Logan said. "I'm sorry about your racket. But look at it this way. Jack's an animal. *And* a puppy. So she does whatever she feels like. I mean, I get just as angry as you do when she messes with *my* stuff. But it isn't, like . . . *personal.* You know? If she sees something she wants to chew, she'll chew it. We just have to put things away. And we have to stop her if we catch her. We have to teach her that it's wrong."

"Makes sense to me," Mom said pointedly.

Logan offered Robert an apologetic smile. He was trying to call a truce, even though smiling for Robert's benefit always made him feel ill.

Robert pushed himself away from the table. The chair screeched on the linoleum.

"All I know is that if we'd gotten the dog I asked for, I'd still have a tennis racket," he said. He dropped his plate into the sink, then strode out of the kitchen.

Logan's jaw tightened. In the space of about three seconds, he'd gone from fantasizing about making peace to fantasizing about ramming that chewed-up tennis racket down Robert's throat so his stomach would explode and guts would fly everywhere.

Logan stared down into Jack's bright, saucerlike brown eyes. How could anybody possibly blame her for chewing on something? She was *supposed* to chew on things. She was a dog. She did whatever felt natural. It was absurd. No, it was beyond absurd. It was incomprehensible. It was . . .

Robert.

Logan came to an important realization at that moment. A monumental realization. *Humongous.* It was the kind of realization that could change you forever; it could give you the power to quit everything and move to a mountaintop and become one of those Shaolin monks who are so wise and enlightened that they don't even have to *eat*—they only have to breathe air.

After four years of struggling to understand the oaf who'd married his mom, Logan still hadn't gotten anywhere. But in less than a week he'd come to understand the newest member of his family better than he'd understood anyone else in his whole life.

And . . .

And there was something very depressing about that.

Letter to the editor published in
The Redmont Daily Standard, June 28

TO THE EDITOR:

While I understand that your newspaper must run advertisements, it was irresponsible of you to publish Rudy Stagg's "open letter." He is clearly trying to frighten people into bringing their business to him. That's not what we need right now. People are scared enough already.

We now estimate that half the dogs in our town are either sick or dead. What's more, the disease has spread to other towns. The CDC is calling it POS, or psychotic outburst syndrome, due to the fact that the dogs always attack someone or something before they die.

The more the CDC knows about the disease, the sooner they'll be able to formulate a response. It's important to go through the proper channels. The CDC needs to track its spread. They need to know when people are bitten so that they can see if they develop the disease. As soon as any new information comes in, they'll let the public know. So here is *my* open letter to Redmont's dog owners: If you call Rudy Stagg or try to deal with a sick dog yourself, you are putting your own life and other people's lives in danger. It's as simple as that.

JOHN VAN WYCK
Redmont County Sheriff

CHAPTER NINE

Westerly wasn't quite sure what he was doing. As a scientist, he was used to planning everything very carefully. Meticulously, in fact. But today, he just couldn't seem to organize his thoughts. He'd left the house after lunch and started walking down the highway. And now, some thirty minutes later, he found himself standing in front of his nearest neighbor's property: a run-down bungalow at the end of a short dirt drive.

The windows were dark. It looked deserted.

I should go home, he said to himself.

He turned around.

No, I shouldn't go home. I've come all this way. I should just ring the doorbell and ask Mrs. Hoover if Daisy is okay. It'll take two minutes. I'll just go up there and knock.

But still, he couldn't move. This sort of paralysis seemed to be happening a lot lately.

In the days following his conversation with Harold Marks, Westerly had felt as if the two sides of his brain were at war. One side kept demanding that he test Jasmine's food for the presence of prions: *Get it over with!* But the other side kept consoling him: *Jasmine's not sick. She can't be sick.* And that was the side he chose to listen to. That was the side that kept him buried in his flu vaccine research. He couldn't afford to get distracted and waste valuable time. He simply couldn't believe the situation was *that* bad. Jasmine seemed to be all right.

Except . . . this morning, she'd nearly fallen down the porch stairs.

But the stairs were tricky. She'd stumbled on them lots of times.

He'd left her at home for a change. In case there was a problem with Daisy.

Just go and ask Mrs. Hoover about her dog!

If Daisy was healthy, Westerly knew that there would be nothing to worry about. It would mean that the disease hadn't spread this far. Jasmine's stumble would have been a coincidence.

He frowned. A siren was approaching.

It grew louder and louder, wailing down the highway.

The next thing he knew, an ambulance was screeching to a halt beside him. At least, it *looked* like an ambulance. But it was all black, and there were no markings on it at all. The back doors flew open. Someone jumped out.

What the—

Westerly's heart lurched. It was a figure in a bulky white safe suit, the kind of full-body protective gear used for dealing with radiation—complete with a helmet and an oxygen tank. Whoever was inside looked like an astronaut. Westerly couldn't even tell if it was a man or a woman. The faceplate was tinted so that you couldn't see through it.

"Move away, please," the figure barked. It was a man's voice, but the sound of it was tinny and muffled, like on a walkie-talkie. "This area is unsafe."

Westerly swallowed. "It is? But—"

"Move it!"

Another safe-suited figure jumped out and ran down the driveway toward the house.

"I don't understand," Westerly said.

The first one took him by the arm and tried to hustle him down the road, his gloved fingers digging into Westerly's flesh. But Westerly refused to budge.

"Can you please explain to me what's going on?" he asked. He wrenched himself free of the man's grip. "Who are you?"

"The CDC." The man shoved his faceplate within inches of Westerly's nose. Westerly found himself staring at his own angry reflection—but it was distorted, as if he were looking at himself through a fishbowl. "You have to leave. The dog on these premises has paws."

"The dog has . . . what?" Westerly asked.

"Paws," the man said. "*P-O-S*. Psychotic outburst syndrome. POS. The disease. Don't you watch the news?"

"I . . ." Westerly didn't know what to say. The truth was, he'd been *avoiding* the news. He didn't want to see or hear anything that would make him more nervous about Jasmine.

"POS is one hundred percent fatal," the man said. "We've just confirmed that humans are susceptible as well. Twenty-nine people have already been infected, all through dog bites. Unless you want to be number thirty, I suggest you move."

Westerly's face went pale. "Humans?" he gasped. "But that's impossible. It's a prion disease. It doesn't spread among different species. There's no way—"

"Aaaaahrgh!"

A terrified shriek silenced him. It came from inside the house.

Seconds later, something exploded through the front door.

Something *big*. And gray. At first, Westerly couldn't even tell what it was. But then he saw the bloody teeth, the slobber, the tail, the pointy ears . . . *Daisy*. She was headed straight for them. Her eyes were glittery, unfocused—two wild marbles rolling around in her head. Her snout was dark and wet.

The CDC man yanked a pistol from a pouch in his safe suit.

"Get down!" he shouted.

Reflexively, Westerly dove to the grass. There were three quick, deafening shots: *pow-pow-pow!* He cringed and glanced up. All three rounds had hit Daisy in the face. She collapsed, even as the noise still echoed down the road—but she kept rolling toward them, side over side, moving too fast to stop right away.

When Daisy finally lay still, she was less than ten feet from them. Blood trickled from the holes in her skull, staining the dirt with ugly, blackish-red drops.

"Is she dead?" the figure near the house asked.

"Yes," the first one answered. "She—"

"Help me!"

Westerly flinched, still too frightened to stand. It was that same voice . . . the one that had screamed. Once again, the door flew open. Mrs. Hoover staggered out. Westerly's stomach rose. He gulped, nearly retching. He hadn't even recognized her. . . . *My God.* She was in bad shape. A large chunk of flesh had been torn from her left shin. The dog had bitten her clear through her jeans, all the way down to the bone. Westerly could see the white fragments there, stained red with blood. Her face was ashen, glazed—in shock.

"Let's get her into the truck," the one with the gun called.

Westerly stared, slack-jawed, as the figure closest to the house escorted Mrs. Hoover into the black ambulance. He felt as if he were watching a movie on fast forward. Everything was happening too quickly. He couldn't sort it out. He glanced back at Daisy. The first CDC man was scooping her into a black plastic body bag. He zipped it up, then dumped the bag into the ambulance and climbed inside.

"Wait!" Westerly said. He pushed himself to his feet. His legs felt like jelly. "Where are you going?"

"Portland University," the guy answered. "If I were you, I'd get home and stay indoors. If you see any stray dogs, make sure your doors are locked—and call us." The doors slammed shut.

"Hey!" Westerly yelled. "Stop! I used to work at Portland—"

There was a squeal of tires. He winced. The ambulance lurched forward and peeled down the road, disappearing around the corner, sirens wailing.

After a minute or so, the sirens faded to silence.

I'm all alone, Westerly thought.

Not that this was anything new. He was always alone. There was a difference, though. For the first time in a long while—seven years, in fact—he didn't *want* to be alone. He wanted someone to help him. He wanted someone to tell him that Jasmine was going to be okay. But he was the only one who could do that. *He* was the only one who could go home and run the test—the one that would tell for certain whether Jasmine was going to live or die.

POS CONFIRMED IN HUMANS

BY SHEILA DAVIS

REDMONT, Oregon, June 30—Psychotic outburst syndrome, or POS, the disease that is destroying the canine population of southern Oregon, is now spreading to human beings, according to the federal Centers for Disease Control and Prevention.

Officials at the CDC confirm that thirty-one people in southern Oregon who have been bitten by sick dogs are now infected with POS. "We have an epidemic on our hands," said one official, who asked not to be identified. "We've already established quarantine centers for sick dogs to remove them from the general population. We are now expanding these centers to accommodate people as well. All owners of sick dogs are now asked to report to their local hospitals or contact the CDC directly. And *all* dog owners should have their dogs examined by their local veterinarians, no matter how healthy they look. We can't afford to take any chances."

Sheriff John Van Wyck of the Redmont County Sheriff's Office echoed the CDC's warning, although he urged people to remain calm. "Remember, the only way you can get infected is by getting bitten by a sick dog," he said in a statement issued late last night. "It is important that we deal with this situation in an orderly fashion. Take your dog to your vet. If you've been bitten, see a doctor. Finally—and I can't stress this enough—do not try to shoot your own dog or hire somebody to do it for you. That's against the law. Call the police or the CDC."

Rudy Stagg, a local dog trainer who has publicly encouraged people to band together to shoot dogs themselves, refused to comment other than to say that his advertisement speaks for itself.

CHAPTER
TEN

"Yo! Logan!"

Logan paused on the rain-slicked sidewalk.

Devon Wallace.

Drizzle pattered on the hood of Logan's windbreaker: *pip-pip-pip*. He shook his head at Jack. What he could really use right now was one of those personalized nuclear rocket backpacks. With two radioactive rocket engines so that he and Jack could blast off this rainy street to a spot above the clouds, where it was nice and dry, and at the same time vaporize Devon Wallace's perfect hair.

"Is that your dog?" Devon yelled, running to catch up. He couldn't run very fast because he was dragging Otis through the rain. Otis didn't look happy about it. He kept trying to turn in the other direction. His collar was stretched so tight that Devon was practically choking him—not that Devon seemed to care. For once, Logan felt sort of sorry for Otis. After all, Otis didn't have any say over who owned him.

"Why'd you get a dog?" Devon asked.

Logan shrugged. "It was Robert's idea."

"Yeah, but why *now*?" Devon asked.

"Why not now?" Logan asked, frowning.

Devon sneered at him. "Because of the dog disease, you idiot. Don't you watch TV?"

Logan furrowed his brow. Actually, he didn't. The sight of Robert in the living room every night, staring at the tube with that lobotomized look on his face . . . well, that had sort of turned Logan off the whole TV-watching thing.

"It's really bad. They say people can get it, too. We're getting Otis checked out this afternoon," Devon said. He peered down at Jack with a slightly curled lip. "So . . . what's his name?"

"It's a she," Logan said. "Her name is Jack."

"Jack? You named a girl dog *Jack*?"

"It was the name of Robert's dog when he was a kid," Logan said. He glanced toward the deli at the end of the block. The neon beer signs glowed red in the wet, gray morning. He could see the deli owner, Mr. Boone, behind the counter. He was reading the paper. He looked dry and cozy. His dog, Thor, sat beside him. Logan could just barely see Thor's pointy ears sticking up from behind the window display of beer cans.

"She's a mutt, huh?" Devon said. "I mean, she's got to be. No purebred dog would look like *that*."

Otis started sniffing Jack's behind. Jack backed away from him. Her ears flattened. It was sort of funny. Judging by the annoyed look on her face, you'd have thought she felt pretty much the same about Otis as Logan did about Devon.

Otis barked.

"No barking," Devon commanded. He yanked Otis away from Jack with a sharp tug on his leash. The chain jangled again. Otis sat on his haunches. His tail was wagging. He tried to get up again, but Devon held the leash fast.

Jack stared at Otis. She growled.

"Your dog is weird," Devon muttered.

"Yeah, well, look, I better get going," Logan said. "I've got to buy some whole milk for Robert's coffee." He started back toward the deli. Jack trotted along by his side, her soggy paws splashing on the sidewalk.

"Dogs aren't allowed in the deli, butt munch," Devon called after him. "Mr. Boone put a sign up a long time ago."

Logan stopped and turned around. "Mr. Boone *has* a dog."

"No duh, Einstein." Devon's lips turned downward. "Thor doesn't get along with other dogs. And there's no way Mr. Boone would even think about letting another dog in there now. Your dog might be sick."

For a second, Logan hesitated on the sidewalk. But then he turned again and started jogging down the block. He refused to worry. Jack wasn't sick. The disease was a Redmont thing. It had nothing to do with him or Pinewood.

"Mr. Boone isn't going to let you in!" Devon yelled.

Sure enough, there was a big sign on the deli's sliding glass double doors. It hung right at eye level. Logan could read it from a good fifteen feet away. NO DOGS ALLOWED.

Funny, he had never noticed it before. Then again, he'd never noticed a *lot* of things before.

Ever since he'd gotten Jack, certain little details of life had suddenly started jumping out at him. Like the way different people behaved with their dogs. Some people controlled their dogs with punishment—Devon Wallace, for example. Other people allowed their dogs to control *them*. Like Mr. Boone.

Not that Logan could blame the guy. If Logan owned Thor, he'd probably have a hard time keeping control, too. Thor was a German shepherd, but he looked more like a wolf. He was huge—maybe a hundred and forty pounds (he definitely weighed more than Logan), with thick, splotchy, brownish-gray fur. His eyes weren't bright and intelligent, like Jack's. They were hard and cold, like two black stones. And when Thor stared at you, you couldn't help wondering: *Is he sizing me up for a meal?*

Logan looked at Thor through the window.

The drizzle was turning into a full-fledged downpour. Logan didn't want to leave Jack out in this cruddy weather.

This is stupid, he thought. Buying whole milk wasn't going to take longer than ten seconds. Mr. Boone could deal with another dog for *ten seconds,* especially if it was raining. Right. Logan hurried forward, pulling Jack along with him. The sliding doors parted with a swish.

The store was bright and warm. Logan wiped his feet on the mat and took a deep breath. His eyes flashed to the refrigerated aisle in the back, the one with all the dairy products. He'd be in and out before Mr. Boone even noticed.

"Hey!" Mr. Boone shouted. "Get that mutt out of here! Can't you read?"

Mr. Boone had never been Logan's biggest fan. Mr. Boone wasn't a big fan of anyone, really. Except Thor. He reminded Logan of Robert, only he was older. He was probably close to sixty. Like Robert, he yelled a lot. He wore the same blue polyester shirt every day—either that, or he had a bunch of shirts that were all exactly alike. His skin was the color of rotten lettuce.

"I'm sorry, Mr. Boone," Logan said. "I saw the sign, but I figured since it's raining and all, and I only have to buy one thing, I could just run in and—"

"Get out!" Mr. Boone shouted.

Logan could see Thor's ears pricking up behind the cash register.

"I promise I won't be long," Logan said. He started toward the dairy case.

Thor barked at him. It was a loud bark. Louder than Jack's, even. Logan stopped.

Thor stood up on his hind legs. He eyed Logan and Jack across the counter with his cold, hungry stare.

Mr. Boone grabbed Thor's thick leather collar to hold him still.

Logan felt nervous. But for some completely unfathomable reason, he laughed. Thor really *did* look as though he wanted to eat Logan and Jack for breakfast. He was actually slobbering. Foamy drool fell from his jowls. He was quivering, too, as if he couldn't contain his excitement at the prospect of tearing both Logan and Jack to shreds.

"I'm not going to tell you again," Mr. Boone said through his teeth, which were clenched under the strain of holding on to Thor's collar. His knuckles turned white. "Get out of here. That dog of yours might be sick. I'm not taking any chances. No way am I going to send Thor to a quarantine center just because some idiot brought his sick dog in here."

"A *what* center?" Logan asked.

"You heard me," Mr. Boone said.

Quarantine center? They were quarantining dogs now? Logan's stomach contracted. This disease thing was getting pretty freaky.

Jack tugged on her leash. She tried to pull Logan toward the counter. She was staring straight at Thor. A low growl rumbled deep in her throat.

"She's not sick," Logan said. "I promise. We had her totally checked out last week. I'll only be a second. My stepdad just wants me to buy him some whole milk for his coffee."

Mr. Boone's face darkened. "Fine," he murmured. "You want to play games with me, go ahead." He flashed a humorless smile, then let go of Thor's collar. "Go get 'em, Thor."

Thor didn't need any more encouragement. With a mighty jump, he sprang over the counter and dove down into the main aisle—skidding halfway across the floor, his front legs splayed in front of him.

Logan's jaw dropped. He couldn't move. He couldn't believe this was happening. He stared in horror as Thor's thick, barrel-like body slammed into a display rack of potato chips and knocked a couple of bags loose. One hit Thor's head. He didn't even seem to notice.

"Jack, run!" Logan shouted.

He sprinted toward the dairy case, clutching the leash as tightly as he could. He wasn't thinking; he was just trying to put as much distance between himself and Thor as possible. Luckily, Jack followed him. Thor came within inches of nipping one of Jack's paws. But he skidded on the muddy linoleum and bumped into a table that had a microwave oven on it. The table's legs wobbled. So did Thor's. He fell on his side.

"Ahh-oooo," he howled.

Logan spun around.

He was at a dead end. His eyes darted to Thor, then to Jack, then to Mr. Boone, then to the sliding glass doors—now fifteen feet away. Thor blocked his exit.

Think, think, think!

Thor was having a hard time getting back up. He kept slipping and falling back down. There was too much water on the floor.

"Go on, boy!" Mr. Boone shouted. "Go on!"

Logan gaped at Mr. Boone. The guy was smiling. *Smiling.* Over the fact that his demon wolf-dog was terrorizing one of his customers.

All at once, a switch flipped inside Logan's brain. *Click!* The frightened part of him shut down. The angry part of him took control.

Something on one of the shelves caught his eye. It was a can of bug spray marked fifty percent off.

The plan came together even before Logan realized it. Sometimes an idea just came to him like a big, soft mallet falling out of the sky—and when it hit, it didn't hurt so much as tickle, and everything suddenly became crystal clear.

"Come on, Thor!" Mr. Boone hollered.

Logan bolted back down the aisle. With his right hand, he held Jack's leash. With his left, he snagged the bug spray. In a single, deft maneuver, he jumped over Thor—and as he landed, he shoved the spray can into the panel that popped open the microwave's door: *ping.*

"Hey!" Mr. Boone yelled. "Get away from there!"

Logan could hear Thor scrabbling to get up. He could practically *feel* those teeth. Jack was straining to get to the sliding doors—as far away from Thor as possible. She pulled the leash tight. But there was no time to worry about all that. Logan tossed the bug spray into the microwave. He slammed the door shut and punched Popcorn, then hit Start. His legs were already in motion.

"Are you out of your mind?" Mr. Boone shrieked.

Logan broke into a full-on sprint.

The sliding doors parted. Logan and Jack flew through them,

picking up speed as they sloshed down the sidewalk. A smile crept across Logan's face. Rain pelted his skin. His legs burned. His lungs felt as if they were about to burst. Jack ran beside him—mouth wide open, as if she were smiling, too. Logan could hear Mr. Boone's muffled voice behind them, although he couldn't understand what Mr. Boone was saying. It sounded like gibberish.

A few seconds later, Logan heard a soft *pop*. More like a *pffft*. Very short. It was followed by the tinkle of shattering glass.

Apparently, the plan had worked.

Logan reached the end of the block and spun around. He doubled over, struggling to catch his breath. Then he looked up.

The plan had worked a little better than expected.

One of the deli's sliding doors was stuck in the closed position. Thor must have hurled himself against it because he lay beside it, in the opening where the other door should have been. A crazy, jagged, spiderweb pattern spread from a six-inch hole in the glass—at about the same height as Thor's snout. A small blaze was raging inside the store. There was a lot of smoke. Mr. Boone was busy trying to put it out with a fire extinguisher. He hadn't stopped yelling, although Logan still couldn't understand what he was saying.

For a second, Logan felt kind of sick. Maybe he should stick around and try to help Mr. Boone put the fire out. . . .

But no, sticking around was a bad idea. Sticking around meant getting into some serious trouble. The kind of trouble that involved fire trucks and cops and a very angry Robert.

So Logan did the only thing left to do.

He took off, running as fast as he could. Jack loped beside him, her tongue hanging out. When he looked down at her, he could have sworn she was grinning.

"Sorry I took so long," Logan called as he opened the front door. "I had to go all the way to the supermarket to get whole milk. Mr. Boone had a little—"

He broke off in midsentence.

Mom and Robert were standing in the hall, side by side. Robert's face was blank. There was no expression—no anger, even. Nothing. But that wasn't what freaked Logan out. What freaked him out was that Mom looked as if she were about to cry. She swallowed a few times. Her lips were trembling.

Jack's leash slipped from Logan's fingers. He clutched the carton of milk against his chest. His hands felt clammy all of a sudden.

"Mr. Boone isn't going to press charges," Robert said.

Logan's insides curled into a painful knot. "Mr. Boone . . ." He left the words hanging. His eyes wandered from Mom to Robert and back again. He didn't even know what he wanted to say. Or if there was anything *to* say.

"I just got off the phone with him," Robert said. "Insurance should cover the fire and door damage. But he's going to have to close up shop for the next few days. Which means he's going to lose money."

Robert's voice was as flat and even as radio static. There was no emotion. Computers spoke with more feeling.

Jack ran upstairs. The leash dragged behind her.

"I can get a job," Logan said. "I can pay him back. I'll take care of it." He hadn't planned on confessing or apologizing, but the offers just exploded from his mouth. *Warning. Flammable. Contents under pressure. Do not expose to high temperatures.* "I mean it. I'm fourteen years old. Maybe I can—"

"Be quiet, Logan," Mom breathed.

"Mom, seriously, I didn't—"

"Enough, Logan," Robert said. "Don't turn this into a production."

A tear slid down Mom's left cheek.

Why are you crying? Logan wanted to shout at her. *Stop it!* A large, painful lump lodged in his throat.

"I'm going to take care of paying Mr. Boone back," Robert said. "That's not the issue. The issue is that you destroyed somebody's property. That's vandalism, Logan. It's a crime. You've gone too far this time."

"Mom, please," Logan croaked.

"You can stop trying to get your mother to side with you," Robert said. "She and I are in full agreement on this."

Logan stiffened. "Full agreement on what?"

Mom sniffed. She turned and hurried into the kitchen. The door swung behind her, back and forth, back and forth . . . until finally it came to a standstill.

"What's going on?" Logan asked. Panic started creeping along his nerves. "What are you talking about?"

"We're sending you to the Blue Mountain Camp for Boys," Robert said.

Logan shook his head. For some reason, all he could think about was Jack. If he went to boot camp, he wouldn't be able to keep training her. And training Jack was about the only thing that didn't make him want to punch somebody in the face or blow up all of Pinewood or run away to Antarctica. It kept him out of the house, away from Robert, away from trouble, away from *everything that made him angry*. "But I thought—"

"We thought you were showing some real improvement," Robert continued, as if Logan hadn't even opened his mouth. "We really did. Your mother thought you were doing well with the dog. And I have to admit, you were staying out of trouble. It seemed you'd made that attitude adjustment we were talking about. But now it's clear to us that you were just plotting your next big move." Robert folded his arms across his chest. His jaw twitched. "You've got problems, Logan. We can't handle you. It's that simple."

Logan stepped forward. "I wasn't plotting anything, Robert," he promised. "I swear. You have to believe me. Mr. Boone ordered Thor to attack Jack."

Robert sighed. He trudged into the kitchen. The door swung shut behind him, too.

"The July session starts Monday," he called. "That gives you three days. I suggest you start packing. And bring your hiking boots. I understand they do a lot of hiking at that place."

Logan could hear Mom crying softly at the kitchen table. He tried to ignore her. "Well, what about Jack?" he yelled. "Who's going to take care of her if I go away? I thought—"

"That's not your concern," Robert interrupted. "Jack will be just fine. *Your* only concern is shaping up. And shaping up fast."

Logan opened his mouth again.

Then he stopped.

What can I do? he asked himself.

It was a good question. What could he possibly do? Go in there and beg and plead and say he was sorry a billion more times? Promise Mom and Robert that he wouldn't get in more trouble?

Yeah. Sure. He didn't even believe that himself. He doubted he could talk, anyway. The lump was taking up all the space in his throat.

Besides, that closed door sent a pretty clear message. It told Logan everything he needed to know: They were in *there,* and Logan was out *here.* Or just *out.* Period. The decision had been made. Mom had given up. Robert had won. He'd gotten Logan the greatest quick fix of all: boot camp. And like he said, it was time to pack.

Right. Well, Logan had better get started, then. Jack could help. She could chew up all the clothes he didn't need to take with him.

"Jack?" he called. "Jack?"

Upstairs, he found Jack in Mom and Robert's bathroom, peeing on the floor.

PART III
JULY 6-JULY 23

CHAPTER
ELEVEN

When Logan first arrived at the Blue Mountain Camp for Boys, he wondered for a second if Robert was playing some kind of practical joke on him. Well, maybe not a *joke*. But as far as Logan could tell, the Blue Mountain Camp for Boys was abandoned.

The entrance was just a gate in a chain-link fence on the side of a dirt road. There was a sign next to it—the kind with movable plastic letters so you can change what it says. The Plexiglas cover was scratched and flecked with mud, and several of the letters had fallen down into the trough at the bottom of the sign. It looked like this:

LUE MOUNT IN   MP FOR   OYS
Est. 1993

When they drove up the bumpy dirt track to the actual camp, Logan wasn't much reassured. On the way they passed two or three long, low, barrackslike buildings squatting among the evergreens. They were built of cinder blocks and painted a sickly, institutional green. Stenciled on the side of each building in red paint was a number: 4, 5, then 6. Vines crawled up the walls, partially covering the numbers.

Robert stopped the car in front of a Quonset hut that stood by itself in a clearing. A flagpole loomed over the building, with a limp American flag hanging from its top.

There wasn't a person in sight.

"Spooky," Logan muttered. He draped an arm around Jack, who'd been sharing the front passenger seat with him. She at least had enjoyed the drive up into the mountains, riding with her head thrust out the open window, ears blowing in the breeze. Robert hadn't wanted to bring her along—he'd said she'd mark up his leather upholstery and slobber all over his clean windows—but when he'd tried to drive away from the house earlier that day, she'd twisted free of Logan's mother's grip and raced after the car, howling. Finally Robert had pulled over and, scowling furiously, allowed Logan to let her in.

Robert opened his door. "Stay here," he snapped as Logan started to open the passenger-side door. "The last thing we need is your dog running wild around here. I'll go in and see where you're supposed to go."

So Logan stayed in the car, his arm still around Jack's neck. She leaned against him, panting gently, gazing out through the windshield. He could feel her heartbeat through his T-shirt, almost as if it were his own.

Logan lolled his head against the seat back and looked out his open window. The morning was still, almost windless, and hot. A few birds chirped. A mosquito buzzed by his ear.

"This might not be so bad," Logan said to Jack.

She cocked an eye at him as if to say, *Don't try to kid a kidder.* Then she went back to gazing out the windshield.

"Then again, it might suck hugely," he added.

Finally, after what felt like ten years, Robert stepped out of the Quonset hut, shaking his head.

"What's going on?" Logan asked.

"You're late, so you missed the orientation hike," Robert muttered—as if it were somehow Logan's fault, even though Logan had had no idea what time he was supposed to arrive. "The rest of the kids won't be back until lunch. Sergeant Bell left a note saying you should wait here. He'll come back and show you around as soon as he's finished giving his opening speech."

"Sergeant Bell?" Logan repeated.

"He's the head of this place." Robert opened the trunk of the car and tossed out Logan's duffel bag. It hit the ground with a thud. "Look, I can't wait around. I've got to get back to work." He slammed the trunk shut and looked Logan in the eye. "So I guess this is it. I hope this does you some good."

Logan shrugged and burrowed his hand into the soft fur on Jack's chest. He doubted being here would do anyone any good, but what point was there in saying that now?

"Destroying somebody's property is never okay, Logan," Robert stated. "Blowing up a microwave oven and causing hundreds of dollars' worth of damage is *never okay.*"

"I know," Logan said. He stepped out of the car and cleared his throat. "Hey, Robert. Will you do me a favor? Will you keep an eye on Jack for me? I'm worried people might think she has that disease and try to do something to her—"

"Don't worry about Jack, Logan," Robert interrupted. "Worry about yourself. We'll see you in four weeks." He got into the car.

Logan threw his arms around Jack's neck and squeezed her until she let out a grunt. "Be good," he whispered in her ear. "I'll come home as soon as I can."

Robert turned the key in the ignition. Jack whimpered softly.

The painful lump came back into Logan's throat as he watched the car speed back down the dirt road, vanishing in a plume of dust. Once again, the air was still and silent.

He was alone.

A strange thought occurred to him. Blue Mountain Camp for Boys wasn't all that far from Newburg. Probably about forty miles. He'd been surprised at how close it was, in fact. He'd thought it would be deep in the mountains, out near where his dad lived. But it was right on the western edge of the Cascade Range. Walking, Logan would probably need about twenty hours to get back home. Maybe longer, since he'd be carrying his duffel bag and stopping to rest and stuff.

It was eleven in the morning now, so he probably wouldn't get back until dawn the next day. It would be hard, lonely, grueling—and a big pain. And maybe that was the whole point.

"Bring your hiking boots," Robert had told him. *"I understand they do a lot of hiking at that place."*

Logan scratched his chin. Robert *was* a weird guy. (To say the least.) And Logan couldn't really see him taking care of Jack for the next four weeks. Or going out to buy his own whole milk. The truth was, in a strange way, Robert *needed* Logan. So maybe he just wanted to scare Logan a little bit. Robert knew Logan liked hiking. So maybe he wanted to make Logan hike so far that he ended up hating it. Maybe Robert figured that a forty-mile march would be enough to convince Logan that blowing up a microwave was *never, ever* okay. . . .

"Moore?"

Somebody was storming down the path. A very short man burst through the underbrush, swatting stray branches out of his way with a stick. He was even shorter than Logan. He couldn't have been more than five and a half feet tall, but he probably weighed close to two hundred pounds—and it was all muscle. He didn't seem to have a neck. His bald head looked as if it had been stuck right on top of his body, like one of those action figures with detachable limbs. He was wearing a tight camouflage T-shirt and baggy fatigues.

"Moore?" he grunted. "Logan Moore?"

Logan nodded. The man had black, beady eyes, like Thor's eyes.

"You're late," the man said irritably. "I told your foster dad to drop you off at nine."

"My foster dad?"

The man's face soured. "Your guardian. Whatever he is."

Logan was puzzled. "You mean my stepfather?"

"Whatever," the man muttered. "We get a lot of fosters here." He tossed the stick aside, then beckoned Logan to follow him.

Logan picked up his duffel bag and hurried after him.

"I don't give an owl's hoot about your home life, either," the man added as he strode along a dirt path toward one of the cinder block buildings. "That's got nothing to do with me. When you're here, you're mine. You obey *my* commands. As of now, the world outside this fence no longer exists. Do I make myself clear?"

Logan just stared at him. *An owl's hoot?*

"Do I make myself clear?" the man barked.

Logan nodded, swallowing. "Yes," he said. "Uh, yes, *sir*," he added. He figured he'd better play it safe. This man definitely seemed like the kind of guy who would insist on being called sir. Especially after the "obey *my* commands" line.

"I am Sergeant Bell," the man said. "That's *B-e-l-l*. As in Liberty Bell. As in the sweet ring of freedom and brotherly love.

From now on, you will be known as Private Moore. Do I make myself clear?"

"Yes, Sergeant Bell," Logan said.

"Yes, Sergeant Bell, *sir*!" Sergeant Bell snapped.

"Yes, Sergeant Bell, sir," Logan said.

Sergeant Bell smiled. "Private Moore, do you know *why* you're a private?" he asked.

"No. No, Sergeant Bell, sir."

"I'll tell you," Sergeant Bell said. "Because privates are the lowliest form of maggot on the planet. There are officers, and there are maggots. I am an officer. You are a maggot. Do you understand now, Private Moore?"

Logan blinked.

"Do you understand now, Private Moore?" Sergeant Bell bellowed.

"Yes, Sergeant Bell, sir," Logan said. "I'm a maggot. Sir."

"Exactly." Sergeant Bell stopped smiling. He pointed down the dirt road toward the gate. "Did you see a sign when you drove in here, Private Moore?" he asked.

Logan nodded. "Yes, Sergeant Bell, sir," he said.

"Notice anything funny about it?"

"Uh . . ." Logan licked his lips. He had a feeling the question was a trick. Sergeant Bell was like the stereotype of the mean drill sergeant from every army movie ever made. Mean drill sergeants always asked trick questions.

"Answer my question, Private Moore!"

"Uh . . . yes. Yes, Sergeant Bell, sir," Logan answered. It was best just to fall for the trick and get it over with. "The sign was missing a few letters. Sir."

"Very good, Private Moore," Sergeant Bell said. He smiled again, pretending to be impressed. "Do you happen to recall which ones?"

Logan tried to picture the sign in his mind. LUE MOUNT IN   MP FOR   OYS. "It's missing *b*, *a*, and *c*, Sergeant Bell, sir," he said.

"That's right, Private Moore. It's missing the ABCs. Why do you think that is?"

"Because it's an old sign, sir?" Logan guessed.

"Because you already *know* your ABCs!" Sergeant Bell barked. "You weren't sent here because you're *stupid*, Private Moore. You were sent here because you're *rotten*. You were sent here to learn how to take orders. To follow rules. Do I make myself clear, Private Moore?"

Logan nodded. "Yes, Sergeant Bell, sir," he said.

"Good," Sergeant Bell said. "Then you and I should get along just fine."

Logan was in cabin three, along with three other maggots.

Twenty-eight kids were attending the July session at the Blue Mountain Camp for Boys, and their ages ranged from eleven to fifteen. Many of them had been in trouble with the law. A few had spent time in juvenile correctional facilities, or kiddie prison, as Sergeant Bell called it. A couple of them were even considered dangerous. On the other hand, a lot of them were just spastic—kids whose parents couldn't handle their wild behavior.

All of them were maggots.

"You got some time to kill until the maggots and the other officers get back from the orientation hike, Private Moore," Sergeant Bell said. He opened the door to cabin three, then stood aside to let

Logan go in. "Your new home. Get settled. I'll inspect your quarters later."

With that, he closed the wooden door, shutting Logan into the dimness.

Logan sniffed. Oddly, the air in here smelled of cigarette smoke. It must be some weird trick of the wind—no way would Sergeant Bell permit one of his maggots to smoke.

His duffel bag lay on the floor beside him. He could feel that annoying lump in his throat again, though he tried to ignore it. He tried to ignore the numb, queasy emptiness in the pit of his stomach. He tried to ignore the annoying voice in the back of his head that kept whispering, *What are you doing here? You don't belong here. This is a mistake. A really bad mistake—like when an innocent guy gets picked out of a lineup for some crime he didn't commit and winds up in the electric chair.* Logan tried to ignore it all because if he paid attention to it . . . well, actually, there was no point in saying *if* again. *If* would get him nowhere. He was stuck. This was real. So he wasn't going to drive himself crazy.

Right. No craziness. No *if.*

There were four bunk beds inside. All of them were neatly made, with yellow pillows and yellow sheets turned down over scratchy-looking gray blankets—except for the bottom bed of the bunk farthest from the steps. That hadn't been made yet. The folded sheets and blankets lay in a pile in the middle of a grimy mattress.

Logan figured the unmade bed was his. He shuffled toward it—then jumped as a light flared from the top bunk against the opposite wall.

He wasn't alone. A kid lay on the top bunk. As Logan stared, the kid lit a cigarette and blew a white plume of smoke at the ceiling. Then he turned his head toward Logan.

"Watcha looking at?" he said.

Logan shrugged.

The kid's face was the color of chalk, except for dark circles under his eyes. He was very, very skinny, with blue eyes and spiky black hair.

"Aren't you supposed to be on the orientation hike?" the kid demanded.

"I was late," Logan said.

The kid took another drag off the cigarette. He had a tattoo on his right forearm: the word *tomb* etched in scary, old-fashioned Gothic lettering.

"What's your name?" the kid asked.

"Logan. Logan Moore."

"I'm Perry," the kid said. He exhaled. "Just Perry."

Logan attempted a smile. "Hey."

"How old are you?"

"Fourteen," Logan said. "How about you?"

"Thirteen," Perry said.

"Really?" Logan said, surprised. "You look older."

Perry's eyes darkened. "When I lie, you'll know it," he said. He swung his legs over the edge of the bunk and sat up straight. Then he stuck his cigarette in his mouth and tapped his tattoo. "See this?"

Logan nodded.

"*T-o-m-b*. Know what that stands for?"

Logan shook his head. He was pretty much fed up with tricks involving letters of the alphabet. He decided not to mention that to Perry, though.

"It stands for 'take out my brothers.' 'Cuz that's what I'll do if I have to. You could be my brother. You could be my best friend. But if I'm in a jam, I'm going to bury *you* in my place. I'm going to take you out." Perry puffed out another big, white cloud. "Get it now?"

"Yeah." Logan began to feel queasy again. But that might have been the cigarette smoke. "So how come *you* aren't on the orientation hike?" he asked.

Perry shrugged. "I wasn't allowed. I got in trouble."

"Wow," Logan said. "Already? It's only the first day."

"Bell busted me for smoking," Perry said.

Logan's eyes narrowed.

"What's Bell going to do if he busts me again?" Perry asked. He sucked hard on the cigarette. "Send me to the Blue Mountain Camp for Boys?"

Logan cracked a smile. That was the smartest thing he'd heard anybody say in a long time.

Perry didn't smile back.

CHAPTER
TWELVE

The most remarkable thing about the Blue Mountain Camp for Boys was that the daily schedule turned out to be exactly the same as the Things I Hate list in Logan's head. Nothing like this had ever happened before. Somebody should have called *Ripley's Believe It or Not!* or maybe *The National Enquirer* because it truly was an unprecedented and historic development, and everything would have been different forever—not just for Logan, but for all people and society at large.

Or not.

Still, Logan was pretty amazed. Life was so much simpler now. There was less to keep track of. The list always read as follows, even on weekends, because there were no weekends at the Blue Mountain Camp for Boys:

THINGS I HATE/A DAY AT CAMP

0530: Reveille (pronounced REH-vuh-lee). A bugle blows. Maggots wake up and make their beds. Beds must be wrinkle free and tucked in with "hospital corners." Perry smokes a cigarette in the outhouse.

0600: Pledge of Allegiance.

0615: Breakfast at Alpha Base. Cornflakes, skim milk, army surplus orange juice.

0700: Cabin inspection. Sergeant Bell sticks a toothbrush in all the "hospital corners" to make sure they're done right. If a particular maggot's bed is not up to snuff, then that particular maggot must clean an outhouse.

0800: Calisthenics. Push-ups. Sit-ups. Jumping jacks. Torture. Anger. Thoughts of taking Sergeant Bell and his underlings—Lieutenants Griggs, Monroe, and Podesky—and stringing them all up on the flagpole.

0900: The morning run. Perry sneaks away for another smoke.

1000: "Outdoor skills." Fishing in creeks. Building fires. Rock climbing. Rappelling. A bunch of other useless garbage taught by the lieutenants, whose combined IQ seems to equal Sergeant Bell's shoe size.

1300: Lunch at Alpha Base. Choice of peanut butter and jelly on cardboard bread or army surplus instant stew.

1400: The obstacle course. Maggots must crawl through mud on their bellies. They must burn their hands on rope ladders. They must scale walls and hurt themselves. More thoughts of anger/revenge—death to Sergeant Bell and his lieutenants—burn down all of Blue Mountain Camp for Boys and smash and destroy everything in a fiery blaze of triumph!

1600: "Work crews." Logan and Perry are assigned to the kitchen to prepare dinner for the other maggots. Perry smokes. Logan cooks army surplus spaghetti.

1800: Dinner at Alpha Base.

1900: Sergeant Bell's evening lecture on the virtues of hard work, discipline, and the United States Marine Corps. War stories from Iraq. Many maggots fall asleep. If they are caught, they must clean an outhouse.

2100: Lights out.

0200: Perry sneaks a final cigarette.

The work crew with Perry definitely won first prize for the most hate-worthy part of the day. Perry would just sit in the kitchen and smoke while Logan feverishly slaved to prepare dinner for all twenty-eight maggots—as well as Sergeant Bell, his lieutenants, and the rest of the staff: a bunch of faceless "officers" who didn't really seem to serve any purpose other than storming around the camp and shouting at the kids.

Perry never lifted a finger. He said that he had no good reason to help. Personally, dinner didn't matter to him. He was fine with skipping it every night.

"It's no sweat if I don't eat," he told Logan. "I can go for days without food."

Logan didn't doubt it. Perry was all skin and bones.

During the work crew, Perry was usually joined by two other smokers: Freeze and Wack Man. Freeze was a chubby black kid with short dreadlocks who swore that he'd killed his principal by impaling him on a water spigot and that he would be happy to impale Logan on any one of the hooks, knives, and other sharp objects in the Alpha Base kitchen. Wack Man was like a shorter version of Perry, only without the tattoo. He had the most demonic-looking green eyes Logan had ever seen on a kid. Logan wondered if Wack Man wore those special colored contact lenses, but he didn't ask. Wack Man also had a nose ring—a slim silver hoop that he would take from his pocket and wear in his left nostril whenever none of the camp staff were around. He told Logan that he liked to store other people's boogers in it.

Freeze and Wack Man were on the "camp maintenance" work crew. While Perry and Logan were supposed to be preparing dinner, Freeze and Wack Man were supposed to be pulling down the vines on the cabins and clearing the dense undergrowth that choked the grounds. They never lifted a finger, either, though. They didn't really have to. Sergeant Bell and the staff always disappeared during the work crew hours. They claimed that they were patrolling the area for diseased wild dogs. According to them, the strange dog disease was spreading fast.

Logan had no idea if this was true. Nobody did. And nobody was interested in asking, since it meant that the campers had the place to themselves and they didn't have to do their assigned work.

It was no wonder the Blue Mountain Camp for Boys looked the way it did.

From what Logan could tell, the only camper who absolutely *had* to do his work was Private Moore. There was supposedly a real cook to help him—a guy named Mr. Frasier. He bought the food and decided what was on the menus. But if he ever did any cooking, Logan didn't know about it. And if Logan didn't make enough dinner in time, the entire camp would go hungry. Then they'd be mad. Then they'd take it out on Logan.

"You better work harder, crap-for-brains," Perry would say as he and Freeze and Wack Man puffed on their cigarettes.

"I don't know what they taught you in dope school," Freeze would add, "but any dope who works that slow is going to get his dopey butt whupped later on. You got mouths to feed."

"Tell us," Wack Man would chime in. "Were you always such a crap-for-brains?"

Logan usually found himself thinking about Jack when they yelled at him. She always knew the perfect way to deal with morons. With Robert, she would pee on his bathroom floor. With Devon Wallace, she would growl at his stupid purebred dog. And with these imbeciles . . . well, knowing Jack, she would probably eat their cigarettes and then maybe bite off their hands and gobble them up for a little snack—and afterward, while they writhed on the floor in agony, she would take a nice nap. And then Logan would finish making dinner and ignore their tortured screams because ignoring bad behavior was the best way to stop it.

But he supposed he should look on the bright side. At least dinner wasn't complicated. There were only three meals. Beef stew one night, spaghetti and meatballs the next, and hot dogs and beans after that. Then the cycle would repeat. It was always the same and in the same order, day in, day out. To help pass the time, Logan also daydreamed about chopping Perry, Freeze, and Wack Man into tiny bits and adding them to the night's recipe. That way he'd have both more food *and* fewer mouths to feed. He could kill two birds with one stone. There might even be enough for Jack to eat the leftovers.

"You know, that hamburger doesn't come from cows," Perry said one afternoon. He blew smoke in Logan's direction. "It's dog meat."

Logan was busy rolling raw hamburger into balls for spaghetti. His hands were moist and gooey. Red juice dripped from his fingers.

"Yo, dope, did you hear what Perry said?" Freeze asked.

"Answer the man, crap-for-brains," Wack Man commanded.

Logan concentrated on the work in front of him. Freeze, Perry, and Wack Man were sitting on a bench on the other side of the counter. All three were smoking. If Logan didn't pay any attention to them, after a while they usually went back to talking among themselves—mostly about how many people they had beaten up or ripped off or impaled. Besides, Logan was too busy to make small talk. He had a lot of cooking to do. He'd only made ten meatballs. Dinner started in an hour and fifteen minutes. He had at least another eight pounds of raw meat to go. He needed about sixty-five balls in all. Then he had to fry them.

"Yo!" Wack Man yelled. "Are you deaf?"

Logan slapped the meat together in his palms: *thwack, thwack!* Ball number eleven was done. It was a fine-looking ball, too, if he said so himself.

"Logan's not deaf," Perry said. "He's just dumb."

That cracked them up for a while. Then Perry went on: "Dog meat ain't so bad. Bell ate it in Iraq during the Gulf War, and he says we should, too. He says it'll toughen us up. A man ain't a man until he eats dog meat. Know what? For once, I think he's right."

"Me too," Freeze said.

"Me three," Wack Man said.

The three of them exchanged high fives.

Logan tried to resist the urge to smile, but he couldn't.

"What's so funny?" Freeze barked.

"Nothing," Logan said. He placed meatball number twelve on the counter next to the other meatballs, then glanced up at the bench. "Hey, can I ask you something? Did you guys all know each other before you got here? I mean, are you, like, old friends or something?"

Nobody answered. Perry's eyes were slits. He took a drag off his cigarette. Freeze and Wack Man sneered at each other. The air filled with smoke.

"That's a dumb thing to say," Freeze muttered.

"Whatever." Logan grabbed another handful of hamburger.

"I don't have any friends," Perry spat. "I've taken them all out. Take out my brothers. Remember?"

Logan shrugged.

"Yo, Logan—look at me," Perry said. "I told you that you would know when I was lying. Does it look like I'm lying right now?"

Logan raised his head. "I have no idea," he said.

Perry stubbed out his cigarette on the kitchen floor. "Well, let me ask you this, then, Logan. Do *you* have any friends?"

Logan finished ball number thirteen. "Not really," he said. "Well . . . I guess I have one."

"Liar," Wack Man said. "A crap-for-brains like you doesn't have any friends."

"What's his name?" Freeze demanded.

"It's a she," Logan said. "Her name is Jack."

Freeze snorted. "A girl named Jack? What is she, a retard like you?"

Logan started in on meatball number fourteen. "No," he said.

"I bet she's imaginary," Wack Man said. "An imaginary girlfriend."

Perry chuckled. Logan concentrated on rolling the gooey meat into tight little balls. But he could feel Perry's eyes on him. They made him nervous.

"I bet she's his pet," Perry said.

Blood rushed to Logan's face. He looked up.

Perry smiled. "She's a dog, isn't she? Wittle Wogan has a doggy fwiend. Isn't that sweet?" His smile suddenly vanished. "Too bad she's dead."

"How would you know?" Logan knew Perry was just yanking his chain, but he couldn't stop himself from asking.

"She's got paws, you dope," Perry said.

Logan blinked at him. "She's got what?"

"Paws. You know, *P-O-S*. What every other dog has. Half the dogs in the state are dead. And I bet Jack is one of 'em."

Logan lowered his gaze to the sloppy, half-formed meatball. He didn't see raw hamburger, though. He saw Perry's guts. He saw Perry's bloody, ruined, chopped-up guts: the same guts that Perry had begged him to spare just seconds ago (*"Please, no, don't!"*) as Logan slowly raised the meat cleaver over Perry's pale white belly and brought it down hard like a guillotine—

"That's why he's got a problem with eating dogs," Freeze said. "He's in love with one."

Logan swallowed. He took a deep breath. "I'm not in love with any dog," he said quietly. "I do have a problem eating them. But I don't have any problem at all eating people. Especially smokers. See, I'm in here for cannibalism."

Perry grinned. "Oh yeah? Then I guess you wouldn't have any problem eating this." He picked up the cigarette butt from the floor, then stood and jammed it into one of the meatballs so that it stuck straight into the air.

Freeze and Wack Man burst out laughing.

"Eat it, crap-for-brains!" Wack Man yelled. "Eat it!"

The kitchen door crashed open. Sergeant Bell and Mr. Frasier barreled into the room. Sergeant Bell's eyes flashed to each of the boys. His face was purple.

"What in the name of Jiminy Cricket is going on here!" Sergeant Bell shouted. "Private Jones! Private Macklin! Get back to your work crew!"

Freeze and Wack Man shuffled out the door.

Sergeant Bell's eyes came to rest on the cigarette butt. His lips twitched. He jerked a finger at it. "Who did this?" he growled.

"Private Moore, sir," Perry answered.

Logan gaped at him.

"Private Moore, is this true?" Sergeant Bell demanded.

Logan shook his head. His jaw started moving, but the words wouldn't come fast enough.

"I told him not to do it, Sergeant Bell, sir," Perry said. "But, see, Private Moore was trying to prove a point by—"

"That's enough, Private Perry," Sergeant Bell interrupted. He fixed his beady eyes on Logan. "Private Moore, you will dispose of that meatball. Then you will finish preparing dinner. Then you will excuse yourself from Alpha Base and spend the rest of the evening cleaning each and every outhouse until twenty-one hundred hours. Do I make myself clear?"

Logan finally managed to close his mouth.

"Do I make myself clear, Private Moore?" Sergeant Bell shouted.

"Yes, sir," Logan choked out.

Sergeant Bell whirled and strode from the room.

Logan watched him go.

Perry snickered. Then he leaned over and patted Logan on the shoulder. "I told you you would know when I was lying," he whispered. "Didn't I, my brother?"

The decision came to Logan quite suddenly, late that same night. He was lying in bed, wiped out and stinky from cleaning the outhouses, when—*bang*—it hit him. It was like another soft mallet that fell from the sky and struck him just hard enough so that he could see (really, truly *see*)—as clearly as if he were standing on a beach on a cloudless day and his future was the wide, green, wavy sea stretching off to infinity.

He was going to leave this place.

Very soon. Tonight. Right now.

There was no reason to stay. Sergeant Bell was right: The outside world didn't exist inside this fence. Logan was beginning to forget what the outside world was *like*. And he wanted to remember. He didn't belong with kids like Perry or Freeze or Wack Man. He couldn't understand them, and he had no interest in trying. They spoke their own secret language, they lived by some freakish code that Logan didn't get, and their twisted lives had nothing to do with anything Logan had ever done or seen or even dreamed about. They made Devon Wallace look like the coolest, most fun, most normal guy on the planet. The kids here didn't even *live* on that planet. They lived in an entirely different universe. Maybe a guy like Sergeant Bell could do something for all the Perrys and Freezes and Wack Men out there. Maybe he could help them, somehow. He almost seemed to *need* them—in the same weird way that Robert had once needed Logan: to pick on, to yell at, to boss around. For all Logan knew, they might need Sergeant Bell, too.

But Logan didn't.

And if Mom and Robert couldn't see that, then he didn't need them, either.

That was really the whole point. He could see *that* now, too. He wasn't so much running away from the Blue Mountain Camp for Boys as he was from the two people who had sent him here. He didn't need them because they didn't need him. Forget "need"; they didn't even *want* him. Why else would they have shipped him off to this place? Logan was what Sergeant Bell called nonessential personnel.

As Logan lay there, he wondered why Mom had taken so long to come around to Robert's point of view. At least Dad had made his decision years ago. He'd just up and vanished into the mountains. And now Logan was going to do the same. He only wished he hadn't wasted so much time cooking spaghetti and dog balls and cleaning outhouses.

Quietly, cautiously, Logan slipped out from under his covers. The cabin was still. The air hummed with the drone of crickets: *dree-dree-dree.* Perry snored lightly in the top bunk. As if in a dream, Logan pulled on his hiking boots and tied the laces. He could barely see what he was doing. For a moment, he thought about swiping Perry's lighter and setting the cabin on fire. Nah . . . he wasn't a killer, even if Perry and Freeze and Wack Man might be. Best just to make a clean getaway. He would need a few supplies, though, to get him wherever he was going. Which was . . .

East. Sure. He would head east. Why not? Toward the rising sun. Toward a new dawn and all the rest of that symbolic, poetic garbage. *Go east, young man.* Or was it: *Go west, young man?* He couldn't remember. Whatever. If it was *west,* that would be even better. He would do the exact opposite of what everyone expected.

But first he was going to sneak home and get Jack. There was no way he would leave her with Robert. No way.

Logan would sneak home, which would take a day or so, and then he would hide outside the house in the dead of night. While Mom and Robert lay sleeping, dreaming about owning a swimming pool or a big house or a purebred Labrador, Logan would slip inside and grab Jack.

Excellent.

Logan crept out of the cabin. The floorboards creaked under his feet. Nobody stirred.

He could see much better once he was outside. The moon was bright, glittering on the flat, broad leaves of the ferns. So. What did he need, exactly? Some food. A knife. Matches, for building a fire. A flashlight. Money would be nice, too—although he doubted he'd be able to find any. Whatever. He could scrounge around for some at home. What else?

A fishing rod, just in case he got lost and needed to find his own food. Rope. Sergeant Bell said that a maggot always needed rope in the woods, although he'd never said why. Logan would figure it out soon enough, he supposed.

Alpha Base was as still and silent as the rest of the camp. Logan tiptoed into the kitchen. In less than thirty seconds, he was able to round up almost everything he needed—including about two pounds of leftover spaghetti in a Tupperware dish marked BELL. He wasn't able to get his hands on a fishing rod, though. Those were locked in a supply shed right next to Sergeant Bell's cabin. But that was no big deal. He wouldn't be in the woods long enough to need a fishing rod, anyway.

Logan dumped the loot into a jumbo black plastic garbage bag. He ran for the fence.

When he got there, he had to smile. Until now, he'd hated every second of the obstacle course—almost as much (but not quite) as his work crew duty. Now he was downright thankful for all that stupid wall scaling. Because a chain-link fence . . . that was a cinch.

There was no hesitation. Logan sealed the plastic bag with a knot, tossed it over the fence, then scrambled up and over himself. The metal rattled: *ka-ching, ka-ching*. He cringed, silently praying that nobody would wake up.

He was breathing hard by the time he landed on the other side, but he'd never felt more awake or alert or alive. He took one last look at the grounds, just to make sure that nobody had heard him.

The place was completely dead. A giant cemetery.

Right then, Logan wanted to scream at it—to shout every single dirty word he'd ever heard or would hear in his life and tell everybody there (Perry most of all) that they were all stupid suckers, and that he *would* have his revenge and vaporize the whole ridge with his most famous and ingenious invention ever, the LMBMCFBNV (the Logan Moore Blue Mountain Camp for Boys Nuclear Vaporizer), and that the act of destruction would be sweeter than the sweetest chocolate cake baked for the richest billionaire on earth. . . .

But he didn't. He just grabbed the bag and ran. That felt pretty good, too.

Jack had been trapped in the dark place for a long, long time. No matter how she barked and scratched at its walls, she couldn't escape.

When the man and the woman had first brought her down here, she'd welcomed the quiet and the cool, damp air. She had no memory of the cave where she'd been born, yet she felt a natural comfort in places like it. But as the confinement stretched on and on, so did her loneliness. It grew to consume her. It was all she knew.

She could hear the man and the woman above her as they walked about their lair. But she never heard the boy. She could still detect his scent on many of the objects in the dark place, but he was gone. The man and the woman provided food and water for her, but nothing else. Not even companionship. They never rewarded her.

They feared her.

Jack could sense their fear in the skittish way they moved. She could sense it in their voices. They no longer walked her. She'd been forced to relieve herself in a corner. Relieving herself in the same place where she slept and ate felt wrong. But she had no choice.

And so she began to dig. She dug to escape—to get out of the dark place and find the boy.

The dirt was hard and compacted. But with effort, it began to crumble. She wore her nails down to nubs. Her paws bled. She refused to stop. She scraped the flesh there until it was little more than tattered shreds of raw, exposed nerves. She ignored the pain. She ignored the froth at her mouth, the thirst, the hunger. She ignored it all.

She would not stop until she was free . . . or dead.

CHAPTER THIRTEEN

Jasmine was dying.

Westerly had no doubts about it anymore. There was no need to bring her to one of the quarantine centers or to run a test from home. Either would simply confirm what he already knew. Sitting here on his rug, unable to work, watching her hour after hour after hour, the horrible truth was quite plain to see.

She had a prion disease.

She'd lost the ability to walk. She couldn't stumble more than a few steps without falling. Her jowls and snout were moist, flecked with white foam. Her eyes darted frantically, unable to focus. And now, as she struggled to sleep, the rest of her body betrayed her as well. She had no control over her back muscles. They danced and jerked and shuddered as if pulled by the invisible strings of a puppeteer.

"You'll sleep soon enough, Jazz," Westerly whispered.

He couldn't believe how fast the disease was destroying her. It was only a matter of time before she stopped moving completely. Then she would enter the second-to-last phase. That comalike sleep. That strange limbo between life and death.

He wouldn't allow her to get to the phase where she attacked. Not because he cared very much whether or not she transmitted the disease to him. But because he didn't want to see the change in her eyes, the lack of recognition, the mad frenzy. He didn't want to remember her that way.

Westerly sniffed and wiped his eyes. He couldn't think about Jasmine anymore. He had to compartmentalize her. He pushed himself to his feet and turned to the computer. Maybe Harold had found that paper. Better still, maybe he had found an immune dog—an animal whose own body could somehow deactivate the prions before they did their deadly work. If there was a way to cure this disease, Westerly knew he would find it there.

But Harold hadn't called or e-mailed since he'd hung up on Westerly weeks ago. If he'd found the paper, he would have forgiven Westerly's rudeness. Westerly's own dog was at risk. Harold wasn't *that* coldhearted.

Although . . . Harold might not even know that Westerly owned a dog.

Of course he didn't. Why would he?

In a flash, Westerly was at the phone, furiously punching in Harold's number. It rang once. Twice. Three times. *Come on. Come on—*

"Harold Marks."

"Harold. It's Craig Westerly."

There was no response.

"Hello?" Westerly said. "Harold?"

"What do you want?" Harold asked. He sounded tired and hoarse.

"I, um . . . I wanted to know if you'd found—"

"Your paper?" Harold interrupted. "No, we haven't. We haven't found an immune dog yet, either. We're a little busy."

Westerly hesitated. "I . . . I'm sorry. I didn't—"

"Sorry?" Harold spat. "That's nice. Thanks. I appreciate it." He spoke much more quickly than usual. "You want to know what's going on? We've got hundreds of sick dogs here and a lot of sick people. I haven't slept in about three days. So if you want to chat, now's not the time."

Westerly clutched the phone. His hands were moist. He glanced at Jasmine, twitching on the rug. "My own dog is sick," he said. "Jasmine." He felt as if he were listening to someone else talk. "Jasmine is her name."

"My dog is sick, too," Harold said. "Cody. A springer spaniel. He's in quarantine. We're trying to get everybody in Oregon to throw out all their dog food. Do you know how hard that is? Nobody . . ." He paused. "Why are you calling me?"

"I . . . I . . . didn't know you owned a dog." Westerly turned away from Jasmine and stared out at the favorite evergreen tree, unable to keep still. He shifted from one foot to the other. It was an overcast, sunless day. The tree looked as grim and skeletal as ever. It looked like death.

"Westerly, are you all right?" Harold's tone sharpened. "Did your dog bite you?"

"No, no." Westerly shook his head. "I just . . ."

"Okay, listen," Harold said. "I'm willing to forget about everything that's happened in the past. I don't know what's going on where you are, but let me tell you what's going on here. People are nervous. We've got lines and lines of dog owners outside the laboratory, and they all want to be examined. We have to put them under quarantine. The ones who are already sick are overcrowding the university hospital—"

Westerly slammed the phone down.

It was a reflex, like kicking after being knocked on the knee. He stared at the receiver. He felt bad. He hadn't been thinking. He just couldn't listen anymore. He knew he'd made a mistake . . . yet some part of him also knew that more talk wouldn't do either of them any good.

Talking only got in the way of doing something.

The trip to Joe Bixby's general store took two and a half hours when Westerly hiked it, sticking to the mountain paths. The drive only took about fifteen minutes. The trouble was, he hadn't sat behind the wheel in well over three years. He had no reason to drive anywhere. Jasmine didn't like riding in cars. They made her nervous.

The beat-up old two-door Honda sat in a ditch at the edge of the dirt drive. Westerly climbed in and turned the key.

It didn't start.

He tried again. All he got was a loud, mechanical stutter, like a person choking.

His jaw tightened. He grabbed the gearshift and put the transmission in neutral, then hopped out and started pushing the car down the road. He groaned and winced under the strain, but gradually the car picked up speed.

Within seconds, he was jogging just to keep up with it. He jumped in and turned the key, and the engine roared to life, belching black smoke.

"Yes!" he whispered, slamming the door.

The muffler rattled the whole way. He didn't pay any attention to the noise, though. He just drove as fast as possible.

Joe Bixby's dog may be immune, he said to himself over and over. *Sam looked healthy the last time I saw him. Sam may be immune. . . .*

He hardly even noticed the caravan of black ambulances passing him in the other direction.

"Westerly. Good golly. Are you all right?"

Westerly stood panting in the doorway. He'd nearly crashed into the place. There were tire marks on the road outside. Bixby must have heard the screech. He squinted at Westerly from behind the counter, his eyebrows knit with concern.

"I'm fine," Westerly breathed. He struggled to get a grip on himself. "Listen, Joe, can I ask you a favor?"

Bixby shrugged. He reached into the pocket of his flannel shirt and pulled out a pack of gum. "I suppose so," he mumbled. "It depends, I guess."

"Is Sam around?" Westerly asked, scanning the aisles. He noticed that all the dog food was gone. Bixby must have gotten word that it was infected.

"Nope." Bixby shook his head. He folded a stick of gum into his mouth and started chewing. "I left him at home today."

"You did? Why?"

"No reason," Bixby said. He stared hard at Westerly. He had a look on his face that Westerly had never seen before. Usually Bixby was polite, smiling—even jovial every now and then. His brown eyes always had a sparkle. Today, that sparkle was gone. He almost looked as if he were about to challenge Westerly to a fight. "What's going on? You think he's got that disease people keep talking about? POS or whatever?"

Westerly shook his head. He started to feel queasy. "Well, I don't know. Is he sick? Does he seem dizzy? Has he been staggering at all? Drooling more than usual?"

Bixby leaned across the counter. He stopped chewing the gum. "You want to tell me what this is about?" he asked.

"It's just . . ." Westerly's mind raced. Sam must be sick. Of course he was. But Westerly had been *counting* on Sam. Sam was the only other dog besides Daisy he knew for miles. He'd seen a couple of other dogs around town over the years, but he'd never met the owners. And yes, it was insane to think that of all the dogs in the world, Sam would somehow be miraculously immune—but Westerly wasn't exactly thinking like a sane person. Not with Jasmine on the rug at home. Just a few weeks ago, Sam had looked so healthy, and Westerly didn't know where else he could possibly turn. . . .

"It's just *what*?" Bixby demanded.

Westerly looked Bixby straight in the eye. "Listen, Joe. I don't know if you know this, but I'm a scientist. I worked with—"

"I know all about it," Bixby interrupted.

Westerly blinked. "You do?"

"Yup. You worked at Portland U., but you got fired. So you moved out here."

Any warm feelings Westerly might have once had for Joe Bixby died right there.

"Look, I want to help Sam and Jasmine, but I need to find a dog that's healthy and get it to Portland University," Westerly said. "Do you know of any?"

Bixby laughed. The sound was brisk and harsh, like a slap. "You really *do* keep to yourself, don't you?" he muttered.

"What do you mean?" Westerly asked. He felt sick to his stomach again, even though he wasn't sure why.

"There aren't any dogs left in this town," Bixby said. He lowered his voice and glanced around the deserted store. "They're all dead.

Either that or they've been rounded up by the government. A couple of folks around here have even taken to shooting dogs or beating them to death because they're scared of getting bit. So if I were you, I wouldn't come around asking a lot of questions about dogs. I'd just keep Jasmine at home and pray."

Westerly turned and bolted out the door.

He could still hear Bixby talking about prayer as he gunned the engine and tore back down the empty highway.

The scent was almost impossible to detect at first, but in time, it grew stronger. Jack's sense of smell was her most powerful tool. A whiff on a fallen tree branch, a sudden shift in the breeze . . . She was getting close. With each footstep, her starved and beaten body begged for a moment's rest. She hadn't slept; she'd barely eaten—just some measly scraps on the side of the road. But her desire to reach the boy overpowered the suffering.

So did her fear.

She was being hunted.

Every human she'd encountered since her escape had threatened her in some way. Some chased her. Some hurled rocks at her. All of them barked at her. The wild was terrifying—even more so than the dark place. She slunk through the shadows, hiding even as she tracked the scent. But the boy would protect her. He would protect her the way he always had. . . .

PREPAREDNESS AND RESPONSE TO POS (PSYCHOTIC OUTBURST SYNDROME)

What should I do if I own a dog?

As of this morning, by emergency order of the governors of California, Oregon, and Washington, you are required to register with the CDC if you own a dog. The CDC will pick up your dog and have it tested for POS at one of the quarantine centers established in these states. A complete list of phone numbers and locations is available on the next page. We continue to receive reports of people hiding their dogs in their basements, hiring people to shoot their dogs, or otherwise trying to keep their dog ownership a secret. It has also been alleged that several towns have formed vigilante groups whose sole purpose is to hunt down dogs. Not only are both these things against the law, they are extremely dangerous.

Where should I go if I'm worried that I'm sick?

Please report immediately to a hospital or quarantine center. If you are incapacitated in any way, call the number below and an ambulance will be sent to pick you up. Hospitals are adjusting as best they can to the sudden surge in demand for care. Patience and restraint are required. You may have heard stories of the public hoarding antibiotics or rabies vaccines. The CDC does not recommend either, as no medicine has yet been proven effective in fighting POS.

CHAPTER FOURTEEN

Crash!

Logan's eyes flew open. He bolted upright.

He had absolutely no idea where he was. Sleep still clung to him in a heavy, uncomfortable way, like wet clothes. He was much too groggy to make any sense of his surroundings. All he saw was gray mist.

Gradually, he realized that his clothes really *were* wet.

He was cold, too. He shivered and blinked. Something had woken him up. A big crash, like a falling tree branch . . .

Oh, right. He remembered now. He was in the woods. Specifically, he was *lost* in the woods. And apparently branches were falling around him.

Great. Just great. In about three seconds, one would probably smack him on the head. It would either kill him or give him life-long amnesia—in which case he would end up wandering into some weird place and getting brainwashed by one of those bizarre, starry-eyed religious cults, the Brothers and Sisters of UFO Eternity or something, and he'd live out the rest of his days with a name like Shadrach, eating wheat germ in a remote mountain compound and never remembering anything.

If he even got that far.

Logan scowled and rubbed his bleary eyes. He blinked until his vision cleared. Being able to see didn't do much good, though. He was still shrouded in fog. He stood up straight and tried to dust off his soggy jeans and T-shirt. That didn't do much good, either. He was damp and filthy. His stomach rumbled. Hunger was starting to pick at him in a pretty irritating way. Thirst, too. (Which was doubly annoying since it was so *wet*.) Sergeant Bell's spaghetti had run out yesterday. At this point, a big bowl of wheat germ didn't even sound so bad.

"So," he whispered. He sounded like an eighty-year-old man. "This is what running away is all about."

For three days, Logan had been stumbling around the mountains with a plastic garbage bag full of worthless junk, trying in vain to figure out which way was *west*—so he could find the stupid dirt road that led back to the highway that could take him home. But no. He couldn't. Because he couldn't find the stupid sun. Leave it to Private Moore, Maggot First Class, to run away the night before a long stretch of lousy weather.

The first day, it had poured. The second day, it had drizzled. And now, well . . . now it just seemed to have settled into a nice thick fog. The sun was still nowhere to be seen, of course. Oh, no. It could be anywhere. Here, there, up, down . . . there was no telling.

If only Jack were with him. All those dumb training books talked about how dogs were supposed to have these built-in homing devices so they could basically sniff their way back home no matter *what* the weather—

Crackle, crackle, crack . . . smash!

Logan flinched. There it was again. This time it sounded like more than just a branch falling. It sounded like a tree. Logan heard the wood splintering as the trunk hit the forest floor.

He didn't get it. Was somebody chopping down trees around

here? Actually, the question was, did the tree choppers have potato chips and soda? Logan grabbed the dripping garbage bag and hurried in the direction of the noise, his feet sinking into the sopping layer of dead leaves and sticks that covered the ground.

The farther he ran, the more the fog started to clear. He also began to notice other sounds: animals scurrying through the brush, the babbling of a stream, the *plop-plop* of something falling into water. . . .

The trees abruptly disappeared.

Logan stopped. He found himself surrounded by stumps.

He stared at them curiously. They were all squat and pointed, like sharpened pencils or a village of miniature tepees. He looked around. A couple of long, skinny tree trunks lay at his feet. Each one looked as though several bites had been taken out of it. They reminded him of half-eaten corn on the cob. He shook his head. If this had been done by a lumberjack, he was the weirdest lumberjack Logan had ever—

Plop-plop.

Logan squinted through the fog toward the stream's edge—just in time to see a furry brown creature with stumpy legs waddle into the water.

Plop-plop.

Beavers. Logan's cracked lips curled in a smile. Of course. What had he been thinking? Oregon was the Beaver State. Not the Weird Lumberjack State. Logan had just never seen any beavers up close, in the wild. Whenever he'd gone hiking in the past, he had always stuck to the trails. Beavers tended to stay away from trails.

He dropped the garbage bag and walked up to the stream.

"Wow," he murmured.

A massive dam had been built across it, maybe thirty feet long and eight feet deep. It was sloppy looking, like a giant bird's nest—with leaves and branches sticking out all over the place—but it did what it was supposed to do. The water level on one side of it was a good three feet higher than the water level on the other side. It was really pretty incredible. That little fur ball he'd just seen was less than half the size of Jack. How could something like *that* create something like *this*?

Logan bent down beside the stream and cupped his hands, slurping up water in big gulps, splashing it all over his face. It tasted cold and fresh. He could feel the wetness going all the way through him. He'd never imagined plain old water could be so good.

When he'd finally had enough, he stood up straight again. He was breathing hard. He felt a little light-headed.

Okay. He wasn't thirsty anymore, but he was still hungry. *Very hungry*. He was probably hungrier than he'd ever been in his life. So hungry that he would even have sunk so low as to eat tuna fish, which he'd always refused to eat on the grounds that it looked and smelled like cat food. Unfortunately, he didn't have any tuna fish.

He glanced back at the garbage bag. He should have risked waking up Sergeant Bell to get a fishing rod. He had no way of catching any fish now, tuna or otherwise.

Unless . . . Logan gnawed on his lip and stared at the beaver dam, thinking.

He was no beaver expert, but the way he figured it, beavers probably didn't build dams so they'd have a nice place to swim. They probably built dams to catch things that flowed downstream. Like fish, for instance.

Or maybe not.

The point was, fish probably *did* get caught in that dam. Which meant that Logan could catch some as well. He just had to make a fishing net.

Logan dashed back to the bag and dumped everything in it onto the ground. Then he took the big carving knife he'd swiped from the Alpha Base kitchen and carefully punched a bunch of tiny holes into the bottom of the bag—about twenty in all, no bigger than the tip of a pen. As soon as he was done, he cut four small pieces of rope, each about as long as a shoelace. (So Sergeant Bell *had* been right about needing rope. Imagine that.)

Then he started hunting for sticks. In less than two minutes he found what he needed: four strong, thick sticks that were all a foot long or so.

Using the pieces of rope, he tied the branches together to form a square. Then he fit the square into the open end of the bag. He punctured the rim of the bag with the sharp ends of the branches and tied a few extra knots in the plastic so that the bag wouldn't fall off the square.

There, Logan said to himself.

Now he had a net: one that was a foot wide and would always stay open. He walked upstream a little way, away from the dam, then tied what remained of the rope—about ten feet—to one of the sticks. With that, he tossed the net into the water.

It landed with a small splash.

The rope stretched tight, like a leash. The force of the current made the end of the bag balloon out behind the square, just like a parachute. *Perfect.* Logan could see it all underwater: a big, empty garbage bag that would soon fill with fish. He had to smile. The LMMFN (Logan Moore Makeshift Fishing Net) wasn't nearly as state-of-the-art as the LMMRC, but it would do the job.

He was in the woods, after all. You had to do what you could.

*   *   *

Within a couple of hours (by Logan's estimate—he wasn't wearing a watch), he'd caught three fish. The LMMFN was a huge success.

As soon as a fish would swim into the bag, he'd yank the bag back to shore. That was the easy part. The hard part was actually getting the fish *out* of the bag. They'd squirm in his fingers and usually slip back into the black plastic netting about a hundred times. Logan ended up getting soaking wet. Then they'd flop around in the dirt beside him for a few minutes until they were dead. Too bad Jack wasn't with him. If she saw those fish flopping around, she'd probably go crazy. He laughed once, remembering the way she'd pounced on the baseball mitt and whipped it around in her jaws. . . .

His smile quickly faded. There was no point in thinking about Jack. If he wanted to see her again, he had to figure out a way to get home first. And if he was going to do that, he had to *eat.*

He dragged the LMMFN from the water.

The fish weren't very big. They were all pretty skinny and less than a foot long. A lot less, actually. Whatever. He wasn't in a position to be picky. There was plenty of meat on them to make a nice breakfast. Or lunch. Or whatever meal it was.

Now the only problem was finding enough dry wood to build a fire.

Man, he thought, frowning. He should have swiped Perry's lighter after all. He had only a single box of kitchen matches, and there weren't that many left. He glanced around the woods. There had to be—

A shadow jumped in the fog.

Logan held his breath.

His pulse quickened. There was some rustling there, some movement maybe a hundred feet away. It was an animal. And it definitely *wasn't* a beaver. It was big, sort of dark . . . a wolf, maybe?

It was coming right toward Logan. Not that fast—but not that slowly, either. It was limping a little, staggering, even . . . it was nothing more than a silhouette with a tail.

A wolflike silhouette.

Logan didn't move. He couldn't. Fear had frozen him solid. *A wolf is stalking me.* The way he saw it, he had two choices. He could dive into the stream, or he could stay still.

The wolf barked.

Wait a second. Logan's pulse snapped into overdrive.

That bark.

It was as if his body had suddenly been jammed into a giant electrical socket and the switch had been thrown. *That bark.* Logan didn't even have to glimpse her bedraggled auburn fur or those liquid brown eyes or those skinny legs. The bark was enough.

But this was impossible. There was no way she could be here—*here*, in the middle of the Cascades—not unless Robert and Mom had somehow tracked him down. Or maybe he was still asleep. . . .

"Jack?" he said. His voice cracked a little.

And then she was jumping on him, wagging her tail, breathing her stinky dog breath right into his face—and he knew he was awake. Dreams didn't include bad breath.

"Okay, girl," he gasped, laughing. "Easy. Easy, there—"

His laughter stopped.

All four of Jack's legs were bloody. They were dotted with oozing sores. Her paws were in tatters. She lay down beside Logan and shuddered a couple of times, panting. Drool fell from her jowls in big white globs. She was a wreck.

"What happened to you, girl?" Logan whispered.

Jack whimpered softly.

"Okay. Okay, don't worry. I'll—"

Crack!

Logan looked up with a start. That wasn't the sound of a tree falling. It was short and sharp and loud, like a rifle shot. It echoed all around him, so that he couldn't tell where it had come from. There was no way Sergeant Bell would come looking for him with a *gun*, was there? The guy was pretty whacked out, but still . . .

Crack!

Something whizzed by Logan's head. A branch on the other side of the stream snapped and fell into the water. *What the—*

Logan ducked down, panting as hard as Jack. His eyes were like saucers. All right. That was a bullet. No doubt about it. He had to stop. To think. Rewind. Start over. If he'd been scared when he thought a wolf was stalking him . . . he didn't know *what* he was now. Actually, that wasn't true. He was on the verge of passing out.

"Hey!" he shouted into the mist. "Don't shoot! Don't shoot!"

Jack whimpered again. She glanced at Logan, then sniffed at the LMMFN. She must have smelled the fish because she crawled right through the opening and curled up inside it.

Several seconds later, two men in hunting caps and orange vests appeared out of the fog.

"Hello?" one of them yelled. "Anybody there?"

"Yeah!" Logan shouted back. He stood up and raised both hands over his head. His knees wobbled. "I'm right here! Don't shoot!"

The men drew closer. Both of them looked angry. And both were carrying rifles.

"What are you doing out here, kid?" one of them asked.

"I, uh . . ." Logan swallowed. It probably wasn't a good idea to tell them he was a runaway. In fact, that would be a very, very stupid idea. "I'm just doing a little fishing. I live . . . I live down the stream a little ways."

"In Mitchell?" the second one asked. He sounded suspicious.

Logan nodded. "Yeah. In Mitchell."

The second guy smirked. "You can put your hands down, kid," he said.

"Oh." Logan managed a nervous laugh. His arms flopped down to his sides.

"Look, it's not safe for you to be around here," the first one said. He didn't look at Logan as he spoke. Instead, his eyes slowly and systematically scanned the woods. "There's a sick dog on the loose. We've been tracking it from the highway. We know it's around here somewhere. We got to take care of it. Put it down. Know what I mean?"

Put it down. It took every ounce of Logan's self-control not to look at the LMMFN. "Um . . . how—how sick is the dog?" he stammered. His voice was shaking.

"It's got POS, boy!" the second one snapped. "And I don't care what the CDC says. It's up to us to take these dogs *out*. The government sure as hell isn't going to do it for us."

Logan shut his mouth. His eyes darted from one guy to the other. He could hardly breathe. His chest felt as if it were about to explode. Thoughts jumped around in his brain like popcorn in a skillet—a swirling, hot, crackling mess. These guys were trying to kill Jack. They thought she had the disease. But so what? Even if she *was* sick (which she wasn't), you couldn't just go around shooting dogs. Could you?

"Have you seen it?" the first guy asked.

"The dog?" Logan said. He shook his head. "No. No, sir. I haven't."

"How long have you been out here?"

"Since early this morning, sir," Logan said. "I haven't seen anything but beavers."

The second guy looked at the LMMFN. "What's that for?" he asked.

Logan's heart was beating so loudly that he was certain they could hear it. "That's for catching fish," he said. He shot a quick glance at the bag. It rattled. "There's a couple in there right now. Big ones." He chuckled, then bit the inside of his cheek to keep the laugh from running away with him. "See them squirming?"

The second guy raised his eyebrows at Logan and grinned. "You use a garbage bag to catch fish? Wouldn't a line and tackle be easier?"

"I can't afford those things," Logan said. It was true, technically. He was broke. And he sure *looked* poor: thin and wet and dirty—not to mention stuck in the middle of nowhere.

"Oh," the guy said. He seemed embarrassed. He turned to his friend. "Well, I don't see that mutt anywhere. I bet it's headed back toward the highway."

Logan nodded. "Yeah, you know, come to think of it, I *did* hear something in the woods a few minutes ago. I thought it was a beaver or a deer. It seemed to be heading toward where you just came from."

The guys looked at each other. Without a word, they started marching back into the fog, away from the stream.

Logan stared at them. *Please, just go away. Please, please, please . . .*

The second guy glanced over his shoulder. "If I were you, kid, I'd head home," he said. "It's dangerous out here."

"Gotcha. I'm on my way home right now. Thanks. Thanks a lot."

He held his breath until they had vanished completely.

Pent-up air exploded from his lungs. He dashed back to the plastic bag and peered inside. Jack appeared to be sleeping . . . but fitfully, as if she was having a nightmare. She wheezed every time her chest rose and fell.

Logan tried to think. So. However she had done it, Jack had found him. *Here.* Forty miles from home, at least. And Robert and Mom were nowhere to be seen. If anything was *Ripley's Believe It or Not!* material, this was it. This was a miracle. An old-timey, parting-of-the-Red-Sea, flat-out miracle.

Too bad he couldn't enjoy the moment.

He had a couple of problems to deal with first. He had a sick, injured dog on his hands. He had two mouths to feed: his and hers. He had no money, no food (okay, three measly fish), and nothing with which to bandage Jack's wounds or clean up her sores. And for all he knew, Jack really *did* have POS.

If she did, he wouldn't let her die. He wouldn't let anyone shoot her, either. He'd nurse her back to health somehow.

And that was the biggest problem. Jack was a runaway, too. Logan couldn't take her to a vet. He couldn't tell anyone about her. Otherwise, they'd both get caught—and he would be shipped back to the Blue Mountain Camp for Boys and she would either be "put down" or taken to a CDC quarantine center. And *then* killed, he was willing to bet.

So he would have to play doctor.

Logan Moore, veterinarian.

Ha, ha, ha. It was almost funny. Almost.

For many days and nights, White Paws had been unable to hunt. It was as if some dark spirit had taken control of his body. He stumbled through the forest, lost and frightened and bewildered—following a scent only to find it gone, chasing an easy victim only to find that he couldn't run.

Sleep was winning its battle. White Paws was too tired to fight it anymore. It settled over him like a thick fog, playing tricks on his mind and body. He had to surrender, to end his hunger and pain. Yet he couldn't keep still. Every time he lay down, his body twitched and jerked. So he would get up and try to hunt again.

He hadn't eaten in a long, long time. He was all alone.

The old pack was gone—dead, their bodies rotting in or around Mother's cave, far away. But his sister, the she-pup . . . she was nearby. She had been in the very spot in which he now stood. He could smell her scent. Great white drops of foam fell from his jowls. He stepped forward—

His legs gave out under him.

He teetered in the mud and collapsed.

This time, he couldn't get up. But there was no need. His sister would find him. He was sick and weak, but she would hunt for both of them.

Sleep finally won its battle, but White Paws was content. The pain and hunger and confusion began to recede, leaving only a warm, empty darkness in their place.

His sister was very, very close. Soon he wouldn't be alone anymore.

PART IV

JULY 24–JULY 27

CHAPTER FIFTEEN

"All right, Jack. I'm taking you for a walk. And I don't care what you say."

Jack glanced up from the crackling fire.

"Come on," Logan ordered.

Jack's tail flickered, but she didn't move. She just put her head back down. Then she closed her eyes and sighed: *"Hrrrm."* It was the kind of happy sigh you would make if you'd just stuffed yourself with a really big lunch and were settling down for a nice siesta.

Logan frowned. Of course she sounded that way. She *had* just eaten a big lunch.

Jack's appetite definitely hadn't been affected by POS or whatever it was. In fact, Logan was beginning to doubt that she was sick at all. Sure, her body was in bad shape, and her legs and paws were all cut up—but the sores were beginning to scab. Logan had used his socks to bandage her. He'd cut them into strips and washed them in the stream and carefully wrapped them around each paw.

Now *she* was wearing socks. And *his* feet were blistering.

Hiking boots and bare feet were not a good combination. In fact, hiking boots and bare feet were about as bad a combination as, say, cigarette butts and meatballs, or bug-spray cans and microwave ovens, or starving kids and stuffed dogs.

"Come on, Jack," Logan said again.

He stood up and glanced at the cloudless blue sky. The sun was high overhead. At least the weather had cleared. The past few days had been gorgeous. No fog. No humidity. Plenty of dry wood for fires. Some people might have said that it was paradise out here. A Garden of Eden. Except that the Garden of Eden probably had other food besides fish.

Yup, out here, wherever they were—near Mitchell, Logan supposed, whatever rinky-dink town *that* was—life was all about fish. Fishville, USA. Fish for breakfast, fish for lunch, and fish for dinner. He'd hoped maybe to find some berries or wild vegetables or something like that, but as it turned out, he had no idea how to find the edible stuff. Nothing looked familiar. The woods were full of mushrooms, but for all he knew, they were all deadly poison. Same with the berries on the bushes.

He'd even thought about trying to catch some beavers, but the beavers had vanished once he and Jack moved in. Their stumps and half-eaten logs and big dam were all that remained of them, like a ghost town.

Now it was just fish.

When Logan wasn't eating fish, he was catching them. Or cleaning them. Or cooking them on a stick. Or feeding them to Jack. And boy, did she love them. She could eat twice as much as he could. Her breath reeked of them. So did his, probably. Why wouldn't it? Every other part of him smelled like fish: his hands, his fingers—even his armpits.

He really, really, *really* wished he had a toothbrush. Rinsing his mouth out with water from the stream just wasn't cutting it. The stream tasted like fish, too.

"Jack, come on!" Logan commanded.

Nothing. Not even a sigh this time.

Logan shook his head. *Enough already.* Jack's unwillingness to move was getting on his nerves. The trouble was, she was a smart dog. She had figured out that there wasn't much reason *to* move, so long as Logan kept stuffing her with fish. No doubt she was perfectly at home out here in the wilderness. Probably a lot more at home than she'd ever been at Logan's house. She was *from* the wilderness.

Unfortunately, Logan wasn't. He'd never felt less at home. Living off the land might be fine for wild animals or Eskimos or the characters in *Huckleberry Finn,* but in Logan's opinion, it stank for a fourteen-year-old kid from Newburg, Oregon. In books, they always made running away seem so easy and exciting. One adventure after another. Nonstop fun. Stowing away on a raft, joining the circus, getting mixed up with Gypsies—that kind of thing. They didn't mention the part about being dirty and wet and smelly all the time. They didn't bring up the fact that you couldn't really sleep—because you were afraid the fire would go out or your dog would run off, or because it was so cold and uncomfortable that sleeping was pretty much impossible, anyway.

That stuff wasn't exciting at all. That was a big pain. Not to mention incredibly boring. In real life, there was nothing to do when you ran away—no gadgets to fiddle with or Gypsies to talk to. . . . Actually, Logan could do without the Gypsies. But he definitely *couldn't* do without socks. Or a toothbrush. Or a hot bath. Or a change of clothes. Or a double cheeseburger with bacon and sautéed mushrooms and a side of fries.

Right. So he had a new plan now. Well, it was actually his old plan, except that he already had Jack.

First, he was going to order Jack off her lazy behind. Second, he was going to sneak home, as he'd planned. But instead of getting Jack, he would take a bath and stuff his face and find the bankbook for his savings account and grab the LMMRC and the LMSCG and maybe even the weed whacker. Third, he was going to buy a bus ticket to some obscure place like Iowa, where no one would ever find him. He could smuggle Jack in his backpack or something. Fourth, he was going to take all his inventions to the patent office, patent them, and sell them. Fifth, he was going to become a millionaire by his fifteenth birthday and live in a castle and devote the rest of his life to destroying the Blue Mountain Camp for Boys and discovering the cure for POS.

He picked up the fish he'd cooked for the journey. He figured there was enough for two days, both for him and for Jack.

"Jack!" he yelled. "Get up!"

She didn't even open her eyes.

Fine, he said to himself. He marched over to the LMMFN and untied the casting rope, then tied it to Jack's collar. Then he yanked it. Hard.

Jack yelped. She staggered to her feet, casting a reproachful glance at him.

"Good girl," Logan mumbled. He hurried into the woods, away from the stream and the fire. Frankly, he needed a change of scenery. The makeshift leash stretched between them. It was like a tug-of-war. Jack just couldn't keep up. She almost tiptoed, raising her legs with each step, as if walking over hot coals. Her tail hung between her legs.

Logan hesitated. *Hmmm.* Her paws must still hurt. Maybe he was being a little hard on her. On the other hand, if she didn't get used to walking now, they might be stuck out here forever. He only had three matches left. If it rained again, they would be in big trouble.

Jack barked. Her neck hairs rose. Her tail shot straight up in the air.

"What is it, girl?" Logan whispered.

She barked again. Her tail started swishing back and forth. He'd never seen it wag so fast. It looked like a windshield wiper.

Logan glanced around the shadowy woods, then back toward the stream. His campfire was half hidden by leaves. It was strange. He'd been lost probably a week now—and until this moment, the forest had never freaked him out. Not even in the middle of the night. It was peaceful at night. He chewed his lip. He didn't believe in the bogeyman or anything like that, but still, he *had* run into two guys with guns. It was sketchy out here. The guys had said it themselves: it wasn't safe. Maybe they were still looking for Jack. Maybe they'd figured out that Logan had lied to them.

Jack scampered forward. She was still hobbling a little bit, but now she was tugging *him.* Logan refused to budge, though. No way. They were staying put until he figured out exactly what was making her so excited.

Something moved in the brush.

Logan held his breath.

There. Maybe fifteen feet away. It moved again. It wasn't a person . . . unless the person was lying down. He strained his eyes. No, it was definitely an animal of some kind, but Logan couldn't tell what it was.

It growled.

Jack's tail stopped wagging. She whimpered.

"What's wrong?" Logan asked her. "Jack, what are you—"

Before he could finish, the animal pounced. The attack was so quick and violent that Logan registered only a blur of motion. It was a dog, a wolf, maybe—Logan didn't get a look at its face. He just saw flashes: matted reddish fur and a pair of outstretched white paws. And jaws: foam-flecked, dripping jaws with sharp teeth that tore into Jack's hind leg with such ferocity that Logan was sure the leg would come right off.

"*No!*" Logan shouted.

All of a sudden, the animal collapsed. There was blood all over the ground—spread across the soil in reddish-black, thick, chunky drops. Logan started shaking. He couldn't think. Jack's screams sent hot bursts of panic shooting through his body. The harshness of it was deafening and unearthly, like a doomsday siren: *"Eee! Eee! Eee! Eee!"*

"Stop it, Jack," Logan whispered frantically. "Stop it!" What if those hunters were nearby again? What if they heard her? "I'll get you help. I swear."

His eyes darted back to the fire, then to the animal. *Whoa.*

This animal was a *dog*. And not just any dog.

With the exception of its white paws, it was a mirror image of Jack.

E-mails sent from Rudy Stagg to
Dr. Harold Marks, July 24–27

To: hmarks@portlanduniversity.edu
From: rudy@rudystagg.com
Date: July 24
Subject: Help

Dr. Marks:

Sheriff Van Wyck told me that you were the expert on POS. I need to see you. A friend asked me to kill his dog and I got bit on the ankle before I could shoot her. The hospitals around here are all filled up. Maybe you've heard of me. I'm famous around here. I don't know why everybody's so mad because if it wasn't for me, the whole town would be sick right now. All I did was try to help. I saved people. Have you found a cure yet? Can I come see you?

To: hmarks@portlanduniversity.edu
From: rudy@rudystagg.com
Date: July 26
Subject: Help

Dr. Marks:

Did you get my e-mail sent July 24? Please respond.

To: hmarks@portlanduniversity.edu
From: rudy@rudystagg.com
Date: July 27
Subject: Help

You are a piece of crap. I hope you get POS.

CHAPTER SIXTEEN

It was almost three days later when Logan finally came across a highway.

Well, it wasn't a highway, exactly. It was more like a deserted two-lane road. Whatever. It was *some* sign of life *somewhere*. And that was good enough. Until this moment, Logan had been pretty sure he was lost for good. He'd been trying to walk west—or what he thought was west, anyway: toward the sun, toward the coast and home and civilization . . . but the woods had just kept getting thicker and thicker, and after a while Logan had pretty much resigned himself to the fact that he and Jack were going to die out in the wilderness.

"Check it out, Jack," Logan whispered. He nearly fell on the smooth black pavement. "A road. We can find help now."

Jack keeled over and lay on her side, panting. But for the first time since she'd been attacked by her mirror image, her tail wagged. Only once. A weak little flicker. But it was something.

Logan swallowed. He glanced at the makeshift leash. The end of the rope was bloody where it had rubbed his palms. Almost every part of his body was scratched or bleeding or aching. Sweat stung his eyes. Strange little flashes danced at the edges of his vision. His clothes looked like Mom's rag pile, only much dirtier and more ripped up. His hunger was like a vacuum cleaner that kept sucking on his stomach, harder and harder and *harder* until everything inside him got shrunken and twisted into a tiny, parched knot.

But he hardly noticed any of that. He hardly noticed anything except Jack. Did she have POS now? Even if she didn't, could she survive with her leg torn up as badly as it was? He was too preoccupied even to make a Things I Hate list, although there was plenty to hate. He hated everything. He hated the fact that he couldn't help her. He hated that he'd been forced to half carry, half drag her through the forest while trying his best to keep flies and mosquitoes off her wounded leg, which was pretty much impossible. He hated the fact that he was too weak to travel more than a few hours each day. He hated that they'd gotten caught in pricker bushes, that branches had lashed their faces, that she'd howled in pain. . . .

Whatever. There was no point in thinking about it anymore. Their luck had just taken a turn for the better. They were on a road. Roads led places. Roads led to cozy beds and hot baths and fresh toothbrushes and big plates of waffles.

Logan glanced in either direction. The air was heavy and silent. The sun was still in front of him, so he figured the road ran north and south. Unfortunately, there were no signs, no houses, nothing—just the same old forest on either side.

A motor hummed in the distance.

Was it coming his way? Logan wondered. Could he risk trying to hitch a ride?

If the people in the car looked sketchy, if they were carrying rifles or wearing hunting gear or anything like that, he and Jack could just head back into the woods.

The motor grew louder. The quiet, steady roar echoed off the mountains. It was coming from the north, at the bottom of the hill, heading up toward the south . . . heading in Logan's direction.

As it approached, he began to worry that even letting anyone see him—let alone trying to hitch a ride—was risky. Way too risky.

He was a fugitive. So was Jack. Crazy mountain men were on a mission to *kill* Jack. If they saw her, they wouldn't just let her disappear. They'd track her. Besides, for all Logan knew, Sergeant Bell or Mom or Robert had called the FBI and *America's Most Wanted* and a fuzzy Xerox of Logan's face was posted in every city from Portland to Miami. *Wanted Dead or Alive! Logan Moore. Age: 14. Crimes: Skipping School, Blowing Up a Microwave, Stealing Spaghetti, Running Away from Boot Camp . . .*

The sound of the motor was close now. Any second, the vehicle would come whipping around the bend. Judging from the volume, Logan figured there was probably more than one.

Yup, definitely more than one. It sounded like trucks.

Heart pounding, Logan scooped Jack into his arms and bolted back into the woods. Branches smacked his nose. He tripped on a root and went tumbling face first into the dirt. Luckily his face was one of the numbest parts of his body, so it didn't hurt that much. Jack whimpered a little as she hit the ground. But she didn't seem all that hurt, either—at least, no worse than before.

Logan twisted around and peered through the branches, still clutching her leash.

An ambulance roared past their hiding place: *Vroooom.*

It was black. Weird. Logan had never seen a black ambulance before. It was followed by another, then another. *Vrooom . . . Vrooom . . .* Those were followed by a huge tractor-trailer.

Oh God. Logan's heart squeezed.

That truck . . . it was like a scene from a nightmare, a vision of something crazy and sickening. The trailer part was one of those open pens used for transporting farm animals. It was sort of like a miniature prison yard on wheels. Only, it wasn't full of cows or sheep. It was packed—no, *stuffed*—with dogs. They were piled on top of one another like gum balls in a gum ball machine. And they all looked dead.

A truck full of dead dogs.

Suddenly, the fact that Jack had been attacked by her exact double didn't seem so weird or scary anymore.

Logan glanced down at Jack. She was facing away from the road, toward the woods. She hadn't seen it. He couldn't help feeling relieved. She'd been through enough. More than enough. Too much. There was even a word for it—when so many bad things happen to you that your head starts getting messed up . . . *traumatized.* Yeah. That was it. Jack had been traumatized plenty already. She didn't need to see that truck.

Logan leaned over and petted the scruff of her neck. She licked his hand. Her tongue was very dry.

"You're thirsty, huh, girl?" he whispered.

She whimpered.

"I know. I know." Logan chewed his lip. He was thirsty, too. And hungry. And confused and mad and spooked and hurting and fed up with this—

He turned back toward the road. Once again, he found himself faced with the exact same question he'd been faced with about a million times in the past week, ever since he'd run away from the Blue Mountain Camp for Boys.

What now?

The answer was still the same. He needed to help Jack. That was the most important thing. She couldn't *walk*. Her leg had practically been chewed off. Even if she didn't have POS, the wound was probably infected by now. And both of them needed food. And water.

One thing he knew now: He'd been right to stay hidden. Obviously, he couldn't risk letting anybody see her. Otherwise, she might end up on one of those trucks.

No. He shook his head, refusing to let himself even think about that.

I'll leave her here, he decided at last. *She'll be safe in the woods.*

He'd have to move her a little farther away from the road, of course. He could tie her to a tree and let her sleep while he followed the road to the closest town. He'd sneak into a store and shoplift what they needed: food, water, first-aid stuff. He'd never stolen anything before, but on the other hand, he already *was* a fugitive.

Besides, he had no choice. Neither did Jack.

Logan picked her up again and fought his way back into the forest—maybe fifty feet or so. He stopped at a nice big pine tree with a sturdy trunk. Perfect. Even if it happened to rain (not that he planned on being gone that long), the branches would provide some shelter. He laid Jack down in the dirt and wrapped the rope around the trunk several times, finishing it off with a tight double knot.

"Okay, girl," he whispered. He bent beside her and stroked her rumpled fur. "I'm going to go find us some food and stuff. All right? You just sleep. I'll be back soon."

She blinked at him. Her eyes were clouded.

Logan stood. For some reason, he was having a hard time catching his breath. His chest felt tight. His eyes stung a little. He wiped his nose with his palm, very hard, then turned and marched back toward the highway.

Jack barked.

"Shhh!" Logan hissed over his shoulder. He kept moving, slapping branches out of his way as he went.

Jack barked again. She wouldn't stop. By the time he reached the road, she was howling.

Shut up, Jack! Logan yelled silently.

He hesitated. A person would be able to hear Jack from the road. *He* could. But she couldn't howl forever. Besides, nobody walked here; they only drove. They wouldn't be able to hear her from inside their cars. Right?

There was no point in even worrying about it. He had to get moving. It was late in the afternoon.

He grabbed the end of his shirt and tore a piece off it. He tied the torn piece around a tree trunk to mark the spot where he'd left Jack. The truck and ambulances were heading south, so—

"Ahh-ooo!"

Logan started walking north. Jack howled and howled. Logan's eyes stung worse than ever. They stung so badly that they started watering. He wiped them with his dirty hands. He didn't get it. Maybe he had allergies.

Yeah. Probably.

After walking for half an hour or so, Logan came across two signs on the side of the road. One said ROUTE 61. The other said DAYVILLE, 1 MILE.

He stared at the words. *Dayville.* Why did that sound familiar?

And then he remembered. He almost laughed.

His father lived in Dayville. Or he had a post office box there, anyway. Logan knew because his mother had had to send the jerk stuff in the mail at various times over the past seven years.

Wow. Logan really *had* gotten lost. Dayville was a good two hours from Newburg, at least. What a weird coincidence. Maybe Logan could drop by and say hi. Wouldn't it be hilarious if he showed up at his father's door, looking and smelling the way he did?

"Hey, Dad, how's it going? Yeah, I'm peachy. Look, Dad, I know I haven't seen you since I was seven years old, but could you give me a toothbrush and a pizza and, like, a thousand bucks—and a bunch of medicine and bandages? Thanks a lot, Dad. Love ya. Don't be a stranger."

Actually, come to think of it, that might not be such a bad idea. Ripping off his father would be better than robbing a store, at least.

Of course, Logan had no idea where in Dayville his father lived. For all he knew, the jerk had moved somewhere else by now. Hey, for all he knew, the jerk was *dead*.

Nah, not dead. Logan would have heard about that.

But the jerk might as well be dead. And judging from the way he'd kept in touch with Logan over the years—meaning not at all— Logan figured chances were good that his father would be extremely unthrilled if Logan happened to pop by for a surprise visit.

Oh, well. Maybe Logan would just get lucky and run into him. Then Logan could tell him what a jerk he was.

He started walking again. In spite of the blisters on his feet (and everything else), he picked up his pace. Ten minutes later he spotted a house a little way up the road. *Finally.*

As Logan drew closer, he saw that it wasn't a house at all. It was even better. It was exactly what he needed. It looked like a house, but the words GENERAL STORE were painted above the door.

Logan ducked into a patch of trees right next to the store's little driveway. Okay. He needed a plan. He'd been lucky so far. Nobody had seen him. Two or three cars had passed him on the way, but he'd just jumped into the woods as soon as he'd heard them coming. Somebody was definitely going to see him now, though. They'd see him the second he set foot inside that door. So he would have to act quickly and quietly—but not rush. He'd have to stuff whatever he could into his pockets and under his dirty, ripped shirt . . . but at the same time not act too nervous or hurried. He had to be calm. As if he were just browsing but, in the end, not buying anything. Which was perfectly natural. Right?

How many people go to a general store in the middle of nowhere and just browse? a mocking little voice asked.

He shook his head. *Can't think that way. Be positive.*

I can do this, Logan said to himself. *This is nothing. I invented a master remote control. Compared to that, this is a piece of cake.*

He took a deep breath, then strolled across the driveway.

A little bell jangled as he opened the door. His stomach rumbled. It smelled incredible inside the store, like fresh bread. He tried not to drool. His eyes scanned the aisles: the cans and bottles and other junk. There seemed to be a lot of fishing bait.

An old guy in a flannel shirt was standing behind the counter at the back, talking on the phone. Logan looked at him. Their eyes met for a moment.

Logan stepped behind one of the shelves. His heart bounced in his chest. *Calm down. Remember: Jack is waiting.* His fingers fumbled for a bottle of spring water. Without thinking, he unscrewed the cap and started guzzling. He couldn't help himself. Besides, what did it matter? He was stealing it, so he might as well enjoy it. The water was like a magic healing potion, spreading cool relief through his body. He actually shivered, it was so good.

". . . yeah, they've pretty much taken care of all the dogs," the guy on the phone was saying. "Yup. All gone. Except for you-know-who, up the road. Don't know what he's done with his dog. Hey, did I tell you what happened the other day? He came in here, looking for Sam."

Logan finished the water in a quiet frenzy of massive gulps, then placed the empty bottle back on the shelf. He tiptoed toward the rows of single-serving canned meals. SpaghettiOs. Ravioli. Vegetable stew. Chicken soup. He couldn't make up his mind. They all looked so good. He was seriously tempted to just open up one of them and scarf it down right there. . . .

". . . if you're in the neighborhood, you might want to stop by," the guy said.

Logan's ears pricked up.

"Oh, no reason. You'll see when you get here." There was a pause. "Yeah. You could say that. Bye." The guy hung up the phone.

Uh-oh. It didn't take a lot of brains to figure out what that little scrap of conversation meant. The only new thing to see in the store was Logan. Not good.

Logan grabbed as many cans as he could carry, then bolted for the exit, cradling them in his arms.

"Can I help you?" the guy called.

Logan kicked open the door. He'd just have to get the bandages and other stuff somewhere else.

"Hey!" the guy shouted. "Come back here! You can't—"

The door swung shut. Logan sprinted across the driveway. The cans jiggled in his arms. A couple of them fell, bouncing on the pavement. Logan hesitated. He fumbled with the rest of them and ended up dropping them, too. They started rolling all over the place. Frantic, Logan scrambled to pick them up. He could hear a car coming.

One of the cans had cracked open, leaking chicken soup. When he tried to grab it, his hands got all covered with soup slime. Now he couldn't pick *anything* up. The car was getting closer. Either he had to leave the cans here, or he had to pick them up. He beat his soupy hands against his thighs in an agony of uncertainty. *Run! Get the cans! Decide, decide, decide!*

Tires screeched in front of him.

Logan glanced up. It was a police car.

He turned back to the store.

The guy from the store was storming across the driveway, pointing his finger at Logan. "There he is!" he yelled. "Arrest him!"

One of the car doors slammed. Logan turned around again.

A pudgy, middle-aged trooper had climbed out and was standing there. He didn't look angry or anything. In fact, he looked sort of amused.

"Well, well, well," the trooper said. "Where do you think *you're* going?"

Logan didn't answer. He couldn't speak.

The trooper glanced at the spilled cans. "Looks like quite a little feast you got there," he said.

"He stole them!" the guy from the store yelled. He stooped and started picking up the cans, muttering to himself. Logan couldn't understand what he was saying. Not that it particularly mattered.

"Is that true?" the cop asked Logan.

Logan shrugged. He felt as if somebody had just punched him in the stomach.

"Okay, then," the cop said. He opened one of the car doors.

"Come with me, son. We'll get this all straightened out at the station, all right?"

For a second, Logan thought about what might happen if he said, *No, that's not all right.* It was a stupid thing to think about, though. He got into the car.

The cop slammed the door behind him.

Logan wondered if Jack was still howling. He tried not to think about that, either.

E-mails sent from Dr. Harold Marks to
Dr. Craig Westerly the afternoon of July 27

From: hmarks@portlanduniversity.edu
To: cwesterly@yahoo.com
Date: July 27
Subject: we need your help

westerly:

you aren't answering your phone. where are you? please come to the university. the situation is deteriorating. most of the staff members are frightened. a few have panicked and quit. as i said before, i am ready to give you your old job back, effective immediately.

From: hmarks@portlanduniversity.edu
To: cwesterly@yahoo.com
Date: July 27
Subject: we need your help

i know you're online because your phone is busy. answer me, westerly. i'm giving you a second chance. you can help us. you can help yourself and your dog. time is running out. i've talked to research facilities as far away as san diego, and they're all experiencing the same thing we are. the situation is critical.

CHAPTER
SEVENTEEN

Jasmine's injection was all prepared. Westerly had loaded the syringe with the necessary combination of drugs two days ago, the same afternoon he'd dug the hole next to their favorite evergreen tree. Everything was ready. A little pinprick and it would be all over, quickly and painlessly. Jasmine wouldn't even notice it. She was asleep. She would just keep sleeping, sinking deeper and deeper into a dreamless slumber from which she would never wake. Her suffering would come to an end.

The needle was sitting on his desk. Right next to the computer. Waiting.

Westerly knew it had to be done. He'd known it for a long time. Yet he had put it off until this moment.

She wasn't a laboratory rat. She wasn't a prisoner. She wasn't the subject of a failed experiment. She was Jasmine.

It has to be done.

Westerly had thought he'd lost all hope a while ago, but it turned out that hope was harder to lose than he'd imagined. It kept popping up here and there, just when he was sure it was gone forever. Maybe the CDC would find an immune dog. Maybe Harold would e-mail him when he had something worthwhile to share, other than his own desperation. Maybe some other scientists somewhere else in the world were already synthesizing a cure. Maybe, maybe, maybe . . . a whole sea of maybes.

But the sea had finally dried up. There were no maybes anymore. There was only certain knowledge: Jasmine was unconscious. In a matter of days, or perhaps hours, she would wake up in a violent rage. She would be unable to control herself. And then she would die.

"I'm doing this for you," Westerly whispered to her. "I'm sorry."

He reached for the syringe.

It didn't take long to fill up the hole and finish packing the dirt. Westerly barely even broke a sweat.

The afternoon air was cool. He looked up at the tree and saw that the tip was just beginning to turn that brief, dazzling shade of purple. Jasmine would have appreciated it.

Westerly gave the small brown mound one last pat with his shovel, then propped the shovel against the tree. For several moments, he debated whether to search for a stone to mark the spot. But in the end, he decided there was no need. The tree—a huge, vibrant, magnificent living thing—was marker enough.

Afternoon melted into night. Westerly hardly noticed the change. He sat on the back porch, the way he always did. He didn't know how long he'd been sitting there when he heard a truck in his driveway. The stars were out, so it must have been a while. The evergreen tree was a dark skeleton.

Doors slammed.

Westerly watched, feeling nothing, as four men in safe suits walked around the side of the house.

"Dr. Westerly?" one of them called.

"You can go home," he said.

They paused in the yard. The porch lights glinted off their black faceplates.

"Excuse me?" another asked.

"You can go home," Westerly said. He stood and leaned over the porch railing. "My dog is dead and buried. I haven't been infected. So there's no reason for you to be here."

"We're not here for the dog," the first one said.

Westerly stared down at them. "Oh?"

"No, sir. We're here for *you*. We're from the university. Dr. Marks sent us."

"Harold?" Westerly smiled faintly. "What does he want?"

"He wanted to check up on you. He was worried that you were sick because you didn't reply to any of his e-mails."

"He was worried, eh?"

"He also said that you'd probably give us a hard time."

Westerly couldn't tell which figure was speaking. Their voices all sounded the same. Lifeless. Mechanical. But then, they were Harold's drones. It was fitting somehow. He imagined that if he lifted those faceplates, he wouldn't even see eyes or noses or mouths. He'd just see a lot of circuitry. And Harold would be at some distant base, controlling them via remote. Control was key for Harold. Control was all that mattered.

"Well, I suppose Dr. Marks was right," Westerly said finally. "I've got a reputation for giving people a hard time. Speaking of which, why are you wearing those suits? Why don't you show me your faces? I won't bite you. I promise."

They turned to one another. Then, slowly, the one in front

reached up and unclipped the clamps that held his helmet on. He pulled the helmet off, revealing a high-cheekboned Asian face and short black hair.

"Listen, Dr. Westerly, we're not here to argue with you," he said. "As you know, the situation is very, very bad. We hope you'll come with us. We need your skills as a research scien—"

"I'll tell you what," Westerly interrupted. "I'll make a deal with you."

"A deal?"

"Yes. Here it is." Westerly took a deep breath. "I want you to go home. I want you to lose your jobs and run out on your families and lose everything you've ever cared about. Then you can come back here and pick me up. And I'll come with you. I promise. Because then we'll have something to talk about. We'll be able to speak the same language."

The man in front shook his head. "I'm sorry," he said to Westerly. "We need you, Dr. Westerly. But I can't force you to come."

"No," Westerly agreed. "You can't."

The group of them stood there staring at him for a minute or two. Then they turned back toward the front of the house.

Westerly sat down again.

Moments later, he heard the doors slam, followed by the sound of the truck as it backed down the driveway and disappeared into the night.

Maybe tomorrow, he would go for a nice long drive himself. It didn't matter where. So long as he didn't walk. He was finished with walking places. From now on, he would drive.

Jasmine had always hated cars.

Jack had never known such terror. It overshadowed even her pain and thirst and hunger. Night had long since fallen, and the boy was still gone. He'd abandoned her. He'd trapped her by tying her to this tree. She howled and howled for him, but he would not come. She chewed on the rope, trying to free herself, but the rope was too strong for her teeth. She whipped it around in her jaw, growling in frustration. Finally she spat it out.

A car was approaching on the highway.

Unlike the others, it moved very slowly. Finally it stopped, its lights glaring directly into the brush where Jack was trapped.

She barked at the terrible brightness.

Men were approaching. She could smell them; she could hear them rustling through the underbrush and barking at each other in their strange, hushed way. But the boy was not among them. Jack barked again—more viciously, warning them to stay away. But the men kept coming. There were three of them. They stood around her in silence.

All of them carried sticks.

Jack stared at them, growling and baring her teeth. She would attack if—

One of the sticks came crashing down on her skull.

White light exploded before her eyes. The pain was swift and devastating. She screamed. Another stick crashed down upon her, then another. She couldn't escape.

Mercifully, it didn't matter. After the next blow, she slipped into a deep, black sleep, and the nightmare faded to nothingness.

CHAPTER
EIGHTEEN

The trooper, Officer McVittie, took Logan to the state police station, which turned out to be on Route 61 about a mile north of Dayville.

The first thing Logan did was take a shower. The shower wasn't very warm, but Logan had to admit it still felt pretty decent. He'd forgotten what it felt like to be clean. To not smell like fish.

After that, they gave him a change of clothes. There was a huge bin full of donated and forgotten stuff right next to the shower room. Officer McVittie chose Logan's outfit for him: a black sweatshirt with the letters *OG* printed on the front, baggy wool socks, and a pair of corduroys that were so wide that they could have easily fit two other kids inside them. Neither the cops nor Logan had a belt, so they gave him a piece of string. Logan had no choice but to use it.

Once Logan was dressed, Officer McVittie handcuffed him to a bench in the main part of the police station.

Logan had never worn handcuffs before. The metal ring was cold and sharp. If he moved at all, it cut off the circulation in his left hand.

"I have some stuff to take care of, Logan," McVittie said, as nicely as ever. "Then I'll be back to ask you some questions, all right?"

No, that's not all right, Logan felt like saying again. *What would be all right is if you'd let me out of here to go get my dog.*

The bench was next to McVittie's desk. A half-eaten tuna sandwich was sitting there on the desk, right beside a newspaper. Logan couldn't help staring at it. His mouth watered. His stomach growled. Loudly.

"Hey, are you hungry?" McVittie asked.

Logan lifted his shoulders. *Were you always a crap-for-brains?*

"I think I can rustle up something for you," McVittie said.

"Really?" Logan asked. He eyed the cop suspiciously. Maybe this was some sort of trick to get him to talk.

"I'll be right back," McVittie said. He disappeared down a hallway.

Logan sighed. If it *was* a trick, there wasn't much he could do about it. He was surrounded. And he was starving.

He glanced around the station. It was small but busy. Phones were ringing. Several cops in state trooper uniforms were bustling around. So were one or two people in regular clothes, the kind of suits Robert wore when he sold cars. There were also a few soldiers, as well as guys in what looked like space suits, only without the helmets. Everybody was shouting at each other or shuffling papers on their desks or shaking their heads. Almost every other word out of their mouths was *POS.*

For some reason, they kept glancing at a small jail cell on the other side of the room. It was full of scraggly guys with bags under their eyes, sprawled on the floor and across benches along the wall. They were all asleep. Logan wondered if he'd end up there with them.

He swallowed and turned to a window. It was already dark outside. An unpleasant ache squeezed at his gut. Maybe Jack was sleeping by now. Sure she was. She'd worn herself out by howling, and then she'd fallen asleep. She was just as tired as he was. She would sleep through the night. And as soon as Logan was free, he would rush back and find her and feed her and bandage her—

"Here you go."

Logan glanced up. Officer McVittie was back. He had a grape soda, a bag of potato chips, and a tuna sandwich. He placed the food on the bench next to Logan.

"Thanks," Logan said.

So it wasn't a trick. McVittie wasn't so bad after all. Logan felt a quick pang of guilt for having doubted the guy.

On the other hand, given his experience with authority figures in uniform—namely, Sergeant Bell and his lieutenants—he really hadn't been able to help himself.

"All right, Logan," McVittie said. "Eat up. I'll be back."

Logan scarfed down the whole sandwich in about three seconds. It tasted like the greatest gourmet meal he'd ever had in his entire life. Then he gobbled up the potato chips. Those were even better. But the more he stuffed himself, the worse he felt. The unpleasant ache didn't go away.

Jack was still out in the woods.

She was alone. Tied to a tree. Barely able to walk. No tuna fish or grape soda for her.

Okay. Enough. Logan had to stop thinking about her. Period. He had to do whatever it took to take his mind off her, at least until he got out of here. His eyes flashed to the newspaper on the cop's desk, a fresh copy of today's *Portland Times*. He started skimming the front page:

POS DEATH TOLL RISES TO 56
CDC URGES ALL DOG OWNERS TO
REPORT TO AREA HOSPITALS

PORTLAND, Oregon, July 27—Autopsies conducted today confirmed that seven more people in the Portland area have died from POS, or psychotic outburst syndrome, the disease that has decimated the canine population across the Pacific Northwest. The official number of human fatalities now stands at 56. Sources at Portland University say they expect this number to rise

Logan stopped right there. Reading the newspaper was probably a stupid idea, given the circumstances. He squirmed and shifted on the bench, searching the desk for something else. . . .

The computer. Hmmm. He could surf the Web. He could check out all those sites that Mom and Robert used to tell him were off-limits. What was the worst that could happen? He was already in jail.

The power was on, but the screen was blank. Logan reached for the keyboard with his right hand. His elbow brushed the half-eaten sandwich. It was a stretch, and his left hand tugged on the stupid handcuffs and made the metal dig painfully into his wrist, but he made it. He tapped the space bar.

The screen winked to life. His eyes narrowed. The computer was opened to some kind of search engine for residents of Dayville. It looked like a blank form. The cursor blinked in a little rectangle marked Full Name, but there wasn't any . . .

Wait a second.

He could find out where his father lived. Maybe he could even *call* his father.

He wasn't kidding around with himself anymore. All of a sudden he was deadly serious. *He was in jail.*

He'd seen enough movies to know that somebody under arrest was allowed one phone call. So Logan could call his father and ask him to go rescue Jack and take her to a vet. His father would do that, wouldn't he? Even after seven years? He wasn't *that* much of a jerk.

Logan pecked at the keys, typing in his dad's full name with his forefinger. Then he pressed Enter.

The computer whirred. The screen shifted.

An address appeared under the rectangle: *Evergreen Drive (4 miles south of town line, unmarked exit off Route 61).*

There was no phone number, though.

Logan frowned. He cast a quick, furtive glance around the station, just to make sure nobody was watching. But nobody was. Everybody had their backs turned to him. There seemed to be some kind of commotion going on in the little cell. One of the scraggly guys had woken up. Or maybe all of them had. Logan couldn't really see.

"Lemme out of here!" a voice shrieked. "Lemme out!"

"Yo!" another guy yelled. "That dude's drooling. Something's wrong!"

"He's got the disease!"

"Get him out!"

"Clear the cell! Clear the cell!"

Suddenly, cops were yelling and running in every direction.

Uh-oh. Logan tried to stand. The metal dug into his wrist. He winced. He could only sort of stoop. He craned his neck to get a better look at the cell and caught a glimpse of one of the scraggly guys. The guy's eyes were rolled back in his head. Big white globs of slobber fell from his lips and dribbled all over his shirt. He was banging on the cell bars. The rest of the scraggly guys were backed against the wall, staring at him.

Logan swallowed. He was trapped in a jail with some freak with a deadly disease. People were panicking. *He* was panicking.

His eyes fell to the desk. With his free hand, he yanked open the top drawer and started rifling through it. Maybe McVittie had left a spare set of handcuff keys lying around.

But there were only pens and paper clips and envelopes in the drawer. Logan shoved it closed, then yanked open the next one. It was completely empty. *Come on, come on.* He bent over as far as possible and opened the bottom drawer. Inside was a bunch of Ziploc plastic pouches marked Evidence in red Magic Marker. Several of the pouches contained handguns. He'd never seen a real handgun up close. They were bigger than he'd imagined.

One of the pouches contained a flashlight. Another had a hunting knife—a big one with a jagged blade, maybe eight inches long and an inch wide. The blade was stained with drops of what looked like rust. Logan shuddered. He could guess what that was.

But the knife looked sharp.

"Stand back, everybody!" a cop shouted. "Stand back!"

"Hurry up!"

"This dude is *bugging out*!"

After another quick glance at the cell, Logan fished the knife out of the plastic pouch. He could feel tuna fish rising in his throat. There was a very good chance he might barf. If shoplifting was such a terrible crime that he had to be handcuffed to a bench, he could only imagine what would happen if he got caught now. Tampering with evidence, trying to escape . . . he'd end up in "kiddie prison." He'd become the next Perry.

Adrenaline pumped through his veins as he sawed furiously on the little chain that connected the two rings of the handcuffs. The blade sliced into the metal with a hideous grinding sound. A spark flew. He didn't know where his energy was coming from. Maybe from the fear of being a smoker and getting a tattoo and spending the rest of his life impaling people and—

Snap!

Logan gasped. He'd done it. He'd cut the cuffs in half.

He was *free*. He stared at the metal ring around his wrist, not quite believing it. The severed chain dangled against his forearm. He almost laughed. He tossed the knife back into the drawer and grabbed the bag with the flashlight.

"Everybody just relax!" a cop yelled.

Logan didn't allow himself so much as a peek at the cell. He simply bolted for the door and out into the darkness. He didn't stop running until he'd reached the highway.

It was only then that he realized he wasn't wearing any shoes.

The torn piece of shirt was still there on the side of the road, just where Logan had left it. The pavement around it sparkled in the moonlight.

Logan breathed a quick sigh of relief. He'd actually made it here faster than expected. He'd jogged most of the way, partly because he was scared of being chased and partly because he was so worried. Jack had to be starving half to death by now.

He should have snagged that half-eaten tuna fish sandwich for her.

"Jack!" Logan whispered into the woods. "I'm back, girl!"

At least she wasn't howling anymore. That was a relief. Logan dug the flashlight out of his borrowed corduroys and struck out into the woods. Like he'd figured, she must have fallen asleep. Good. She could use the rest.

The powerful beam of light danced through the branches as he plowed forward. "Jack, wake up, girl! It's me!"

It hadn't been so bad running in socks on the pavement, but now Logan winced every time he took a step. Needles and twigs and stones stabbed through the fabric. Whatever. He could take it. He was going to come right back to the highway, anyway.

He had a new plan now. He was going to Dad's house.

He'd finally get to see the hot tub and trampoline. He figured he was . . . what? Already two miles south of the town line? Maybe even farther. So he had two more miles to go at most. On pavement. No sweat.

He could see the pine tree a few yards ahead of him. "Hey, Jack!" he called again, a little louder. She wasn't even barking. At home she always barked when Logan returned after being gone for a while. She must really be wiped out.

"Jack?" He looked down.

At first, he didn't even recognize the bloody body on the ground in front of him. He thought it might be some kind of animal that Jack had managed to kill and partially devour.

But the animal was tied to the tree with the rope.

"Oh my God," Logan breathed.

The flashlight slipped from his fingers.

He fell to his knees and picked it up. He started searching Jack's body with the light for any sign of life. All he saw was blood. He started shaking. Invisible burning tentacles seized his stomach, twisting and squeezing it. She'd been attacked. Something had torn her to pieces. Something had—

Wait.

A wheeze. A very faint wheeze.

Logan put his ear to her fur. Yes, there was life there: a muted heartbeat, lungs struggling to breathe. He wiped her blood off his face with his sweatshirt sleeve, then untied the rope with shaking fingers. He scooped her into his arms. He didn't bother taking the flashlight with him. The moon had gotten him this far. It would take him the rest of the way.

One hour, two hours . . . Logan had no idea how long he'd been carrying Jack. Dad's house must be close, but he hadn't seen anything that looked like an unmarked exit.

Somewhere in the middle of the night, on that deserted road, he knew that he had to rest. Every twenty paces, he yawned. His back and arms could no longer support Jack's weight. Drowsiness had been tempting him for a long while. Now it was like a warm, fuzzy blanket that he could no longer resist. He couldn't *afford* to resist it. He'd close his eyes—just for a second, just to rest them— and end up nearly stumbling and dropping her.

He was putting Jack's life in danger. He *had* to stop.

He was even starting to see things . . . blurred, flickering lights—something glowing in the forest. *Forget it,* he said to himself. There was no point in going on. Not like this. He'd curl up on the side of the road and take a nap. Just for a little bit.

There was a ditch up ahead. A beat-up old car was parked in it. Logan sank down beside the car. He laid Jack on the gravel, then stretched out next to her. His joints creaked. Using his hands for a pillow, he made himself as comfortable as he could.

He'd never imagined gravel could feel so soft.

PART V

JULY 28

Top-secret orders given to the Oregon National Guard, posted the morning of July 28

Communiqué 776 Encrypted 15—Integer Scramble
Zone 1, Oregon

To: Garfield, Commanding
From: Eagle's Nest
Re: Operation Wolf

Follows: CONFIRM ORDERS TO NEUTRALIZE ALL DOGS IN ZONE 1. ANY ATTEMPT TO INTERFERE WITH NEUTRAL-IZATION PROCEDURE MAY BE CONSIDERED AN ACT OF SEDITION AND A CRIME AGAINST THE UNITED STATES OF AMERICA. CONFIRM ORDERS TO QUARANTINE ALL DOG OWNERS EFFECTIVE IMMEDIATELY, WITHOUT EXCEPTION.

CHAPTER NINETEEN

Logan should have been used to waking up in strange places without the slightest idea of what was going on. But he wasn't. It wasn't the kind of thing you could get the hang of and say, *Oh, yeah. My life is one never-ending freak show. I get it now.*

Nope. No matter how many times it happened, he still felt just as spooked.

The first thing he noticed was that he was lying on something soft. And wherever he was, it was very, very bright. A little *too* bright. Logan rubbed his eyes. It looked like a bedroom, small and sparsely furnished. He was under the covers . . . a red-and-white-checked quilt.

Aside from the quilt, all he could see was a dresser. The dresser was made from the same unfinished wood as the walls and floor. There were no pictures, no plants—nothing except a small clock on the dresser.

Logan squinted at it. It was almost twelve o'clock.

Aha. Right then, he figured out why it was so bright. There was a skylight directly over the bed. And the sun was right smack in the middle of it, beating down on him.

That was a start, anyway.

So. He was in a house. (At least, it seemed like a house.) It was noon. He just needed to piece everything else together. He would stop being spooked as soon as he sorted it all out.

First things first. His left arm hurt. His wrist hurt, too, where the handcuff was, but this new pain was higher, near his biceps. It was all swollen and achy there. Maybe he'd bumped it.

He sat up in the bed and rubbed his eyes again, very hard. Memories drifted like dust motes through his mind, but he was having a hard time separating what he'd dreamed from what he'd actually done. Lying down in a road, seeing a shadow standing over him . . . It was more like a bunch of impressions, really—like those paintings that are made up of lots of little dots. You can't really form a clear picture until you're very, very far away—

The bedroom door opened. A man stepped into the room.

Dad.

No question. There he was, in the flesh. Right in front of him. So Logan had found him after all. Or he'd found Logan. Or *something.*

The jerk looked pretty much the same as Logan remembered, except his hair was longer and grayer. It was tied into a ponytail. His face was a little thinner. He had more scruff on his cheeks, too. He was wearing jeans and a sweatshirt—pretty much the exact same outfit he'd worn when he'd walked out on Mom and Logan seven years ago.

Well. If anything felt like a dream, *this* did.

The clock ticked: *ticktock, ticktock.* Logan stared at his father. He felt nothing. He was absolutely blank. It sort of freaked him out. He should be shocked. He should burst into tears. He should clamp his hands against the sides of his head and say, *"Oh my God!"* This was a pretty big deal, as far as big deals went—right up there with getting sent to boot camp and escaping from jail and inventing a nuclear vaporizer that could destroy everything he hated.

Logan *knew* it was a big deal. He just couldn't *experience* it.

One minute, he was lying down in a ditch. The next, he was

waking up to be reunited with his father. But he felt as though he were reading about it in a boring novel he'd been assigned for homework. His mind put the pieces together in a dull, detached way—as if it were performing a chore. *The ditch must be close to Dad's house. He found you on the road and took you in. He put you to bed. And now he's here, looking at you. Looking, and looking, and looking . . .*

Logan frowned. Maybe *he* should say something. Then maybe some sort of emotion would kick in.

"How's it going, Dad?" he asked. His voice was hoarse from sleep.

His father blinked. He even tried to smile, but it didn't quite work. He just ended up sort of cringing, as if he had a bad toothache.

"I'm sorry, young man," Dad said. Funny. His tone was just how Logan remembered it. Deep and gravelly and formal.

"I think you must be a little disoriented. You've obviously been through some trauma. I'm not your father. My name is Dr. Craig Westerly. I found you on the edge of my property, and—"

"You *are* my father, you jerk. It's me. Logan."

Dad blinked again. His face went pale. Logan could actually *see* his skin change color.

"Logan?" Dad breathed.

Logan nodded. "That's the name you gave me," he said. "Although I'm not surprised you don't recognize my face. I've changed a little since I was seven."

Dad clutched the door frame. He looked as if he were about to fall over. His mouth opened, then closed, then opened again.

"How did you find me?" he finally gasped.

Logan scowled at him. That was it? That was the only thing he could think of to say? No *My, how you've grown!* No *Gee, Logan, I'm sorry for running out on you.* Not even a *How's tricks, kid?* No. Of course not. What did Logan expect? This wasn't a normal human being. This was his father.

"The state police," Logan said.

"The police? I don't understand. Is that why you're wearing those broken handcuffs? I don't understand—"

"It's kind of a long story. See, I was with my dog, and—" He broke off in midsentence, suddenly seized with panic. His eyes darted around the room. He tossed the covers aside. "Jack! Where's Jack?"

"Where's who?"

"My *dog*!"

"She's outside," Dad said. "I don't understand—"

"What are you, slow?" Logan interrupted. "All you seem to be able to say is 'I don't understand.' Aren't you supposed to be some kind of genius scientist?"

Dad shook his head. "I—"

"Why is Jack outside?" Logan demanded in his loudest voice.

"Well, as I was saying, I found you both this morning at the edge of my property. The dog was hurt. Very badly beaten. And bloody. And given all the worry about POS, you know, I couldn't handle her until I put on protective gear—"

"Get to the point," Logan spat.

"She's out on the porch," Dad said.

"Is she alive?"

Dad nodded. "Last time I checked. I gave her some food and water. But she's pretty far gone."

"And it never occurred to you to take her to the vet or the CDC?"

Dad's face started regaining some of its color. He straightened. His lips pressed into a tight line. "Logan, they won't help your dog. Don't you know how they're handling dogs because of POS?

And frankly, given the condition *you* were in, I had to prioritize."

Logan's eyes narrowed. "What are you talking about?"

"I tested you for POS while you were asleep. If you notice that your arm is a little tender, it's from an injection I used to dye your blood. I had to take a sample and examine it under a microscope to make sure—"

"Hold it. Stop right there." Logan stared straight into his father's eyes. "You *dyed* my blood? While I was asleep? Without telling me?"

Dad shrugged calmly. "It's a harmless procedure."

At last, Logan was feeling some emotion. The name of this particular emotion was *anger*. The kind of anger that drove people to conquer and kill and destroy and pillage. "So if you tested me, why didn't you test Jack?" he demanded.

Dad tilted his head, looking puzzled. "Well, because she's already sick, Logan. Isn't it obvious?"

"She is *not* sick," Logan shot back. "She just needs help. She was attacked."

Dad met his stare. "How do you know she's not sick?"

"I just know," Logan muttered.

"You know that she was bitten, don't you?"

"So what?"

"That's how dogs are infected," Dad said.

"Well, *she* wasn't infected," Logan said stubbornly. A vivid image flashed through his mind—that of Jack's mysterious twin, leaping through the air and wrapping those jaws around her leg.

"What kind of food does she eat?"

"I don't *know*, Dad." Logan groaned. "Dog food. What difference does it make?"

"None, I suppose," Dad mumbled. He stroked his chin. "All right. If it'll make you feel better, I'll test her. But then we're taking you to a hospital, all right? You're malnourished and dehydrated at the very least. You need to be properly checked out."

Logan didn't answer. He wasn't even sure if he *wanted* Jack to be tested. Maybe it was better not to know. Maybe it was better just to cling to the hope that she wasn't sick.

Dad hesitated in the doorway. "What does 'OG' stand for?" he asked.

Logan glared at him. "What?"

"Your shirt." Dad pointed at Logan's chest. "It says 'OG.'"

"Oh." Logan flopped back down on the bed and closed his eyes. "I don't know. The cops gave it to me. My other clothes were ruined."

Dad laughed softly. "Probably stands for 'Old Grouch.'" He closed the door and headed downstairs.

Logan frowned. Then he laughed, too. He didn't know why. Nothing was funny about that stupid, moronic, lame little comment.

In fact, nothing was funny at all. Period.

CHAPTER
TWENTY

Westerly hadn't asked for any of this.

He hadn't asked for the sudden family reunion. He hadn't asked to go to his car this morning—for the sole purpose of taking a drive to get his mind off Jasmine—only to find a starving boy and his dog lying next to his car. He certainly hadn't asked for that boy to be his *son*. Most of all, he hadn't asked for . . .

He shoved his eyes back against the microscope's dual eyepieces.

This couldn't be happening. But it was. He'd only agreed to test the dog to indulge Logan's wish so that the boy would agree to go to a hospital.

Westerly had never once imagined he would see what he was seeing right now.

Or rather, what he *wasn't* seeing.

Prion diseases left telltale signs in an animal's tissue—specifically, black, star-shaped spots called astrogliosis. As the infection spread, these spots started clogging the animal's brain. That was why the animal began to tremble and drool. That was why it lost its balance. That was why its body eventually shut down. The psychotic outbursts of POS were probably caused by something else—but no doubt the clogging in the brain played a part.

Yet this dog's tissue showed no signs of astrogliosis.

None. Not a single star-shaped spot.

Westerly blinked. Maybe this was some kind of punishment. As a scientist, he didn't believe in the supernatural—but this dog's tissue might just change his opinion. What other possible explanation could there be? Some unseen force was testing him, torturing him, making him pay for all the terrible mistakes he'd made. It was like a cruel fable, a legend from some forgotten religion. A man loses everything. He buries the only creature he ever truly loved. And the very next day, as if by magic, his long-lost son walks back into his life, bearing the one gift that could possibly have saved that creature's life.

Of course, *possibly* was the key word. Chances were that Jasmine would have died before a treatment could have been developed, anyway. And Westerly still wasn't quite one hundred percent sure about the health of this . . . *Jack.*

But with each passing second, he grew more and more certain.

He'd been examining her tissue for over an hour now. He'd drawn three separate samples from three different parts of her body: the leg that had been bitten, her chest, and the area between her shoulder blades. All looked the same. Clean. Spotless. Even the blood surrounding the bite was uninfected by the usual bacteria.

The clincher was that the animal that had bitten her—another dog, it seemed—had left traces of *its* blood in her leg. And *that* blood was infected.

But not hers.

There could really be no doubt anymore. Aside from the injuries (which were substantial: cuts, bruises, a crushed collarbone, and several broken ribs) . . . aside from those, Logan's dog was perfectly healthy.

Perfectly healthy.

Westerly pushed the microscope away from him.

"So. Where's the hot tub and trampoline?"

He whirled around. Logan was standing right behind him. Westerly hadn't even heard him come downstairs.

"What?" Westerly asked.

"Never mind," Logan murmured. "Inside joke."

"Please don't sneak up on me like that. You scared me."

"Sorry," Logan said. "It just looked like you'd finished whatever you were doing."

Westerly glanced at Jack, lying on the rug—the rug where Jasmine *should* have been lying. Jack was wheezing. Her broken ribs made it hard for her to breathe.

"So what's the story? Is she sick?" Logan asked.

"No, Logan," Westerly stated quietly. "Your dog is immune to POS."

Logan looked up. His eyes brightened. "Really? See. I told you she wasn't sick."

For the briefest moment, the relief on his son's face washed away the anger he felt toward the dog. But then, for some reason Westerly couldn't identify, that very same happiness made him even *more* angry. "I just told you that your dog is immune to POS, Logan. Do you understand the significance of that?"

"Uh . . . yeah." Logan seemed puzzled. "It means we can take her to a vet and get her fixed up."

Westerly shook his head. "No, we can't," he said.

"Why not?"

"Because the CDC will dispose of her, if the state troopers don't get to her first. Don't you read the papers? Don't you follow the news at all?"

Logan's face darkened. "Actually, Dad, I don't. See, Mom and Robert sent me to boot camp, and then I ran away, and then I got lost in the woods for about a week, and then I was arrested for shoplifting." His voice quickly rose to a shout. The veins in his scrawny neck bulged. *"So, no. I haven't had time to read the stupid papers!"*

Westerly swallowed. He had no idea what to make of what Logan had just said. If it was the truth . . . well, if it was the truth, then Westerly knew he should have made more of an effort to keep tabs on his ex-wife. *Boot camp?* What did that mean—that in the past seven years, his son had turned into some kind of juvenile delinquent? He couldn't believe it. No, correction . . . what he *really* couldn't believe was that seven years ago, Logan's mother had actually had the nerve to accuse *him* of being a bad parent, of being a quitter, of wallowing in self-pity after losing his job and neglecting his family. . . .

Okay, so maybe he *had* felt a little sorry for himself. But one thing was certain: He would have never allowed Logan to turn out like this. Not if he'd had anything to say about how the boy was raised.

"Why are we even standing around here?" Logan asked. "If I'm supposed to take Jack to a hospital, why aren't we doing that right now?"

"Because there's no point," Westerly said, trying to be patient.

"What are you talking about?" Logan said. "She needs help!"

"That's true," Westerly said. "She needs some basic medical care and a lot of rest. I can provide that for her right here. I have everything . . . everything we need." He choked on the last three words. Over the years, he'd stockpiled lots of veterinary equipment so that he could tend to Jasmine at home if she were ever sick or injured. He'd collected enough surgical tools and bandages and medicine to open a small animal hospital.

And in the end, none of it had done a bit of good.

"So why don't you just get to work?" Logan pressed. "Why don't you *do* something? My dog is dying, Dad! Come on!"

Westerly stared at him. "You know, your dog could have saved my dog's life," he said. His voice quavered. He turned away from Logan and sat at his desk.

Logan didn't say anything for a while.

"You had a dog?" he asked finally.

"Yes. I did. She died yesterday."

"Oh. I'm sorry." Logan cleared his throat. "But, you know, I have no idea what you're talking about. How could my dog have saved your dog's life?"

"Because your dog is immune, Logan," Westerly said. "Your dog is one in a million. And if I'd gotten my hands on her, I could have taken her to the university and gotten to work on a cure. I could have used her tissue to create an antidote."

Again, Logan was silent. Westerly could feel tears welling in his eyes. He fought them back. He refused to cry in front of his son.

"Why are you mad at me?" Logan asked.

Westerly spun around in his chair. "What?"

"You're acting as if I was supposed to know all this. How was I supposed to know? How was I even supposed to know you had a *dog*? We haven't spoken to each other in seven years, remember? Not since you walked out on us."

Westerly didn't answer. He closed his eyes and rubbed his temples. His head was suddenly throbbing. He couldn't take the stress of this encounter anymore. He and his son weren't communicating. In a way, this conversation was very similar to the last conversation he'd had with Logan's mother. *She* hadn't been able to understand why he'd been too miserable to explain himself, either.

Maybe he should just call her and have her come pick Logan up. The boy was on the run; he was wearing a broken handcuff. Trying to help him was asking for trouble, clearly. Marianne could take him to the hospital nearest to Pinewood. Westerly would tend to this dog, but the less he got involved with Logan's problems, the better.

"You know, Mom was right," Logan said. "You really are a quitter."

Westerly opened his eyes. "Excuse me?"

"You heard me. Listen to what you're saying. You're not making any sense. You won't take my dog to the hospital. But you said that if you *did,* you would use her to help create a cure. I don't get it. Just because *your* dog is dead, every other dog has to die, too? Is that it? You're just giving up again? The way you gave up on Mom and me?"

Abruptly, Westerly was seething with rage. If anything, Logan and his mother had given up on *him.* "How dare you talk to me like that?" he snapped.

Logan sneered. "I can talk to you however I want," he said.

"No, you cannot! I am an adult! You are a child!"

"So what?" Logan said. He laughed grimly. "What's the difference? Every adult I've ever met is just as lame and stupid and selfish as every kid I've ever met. The adults are just allowed to get away with it." He bent down and scooped Jack into his arms. "You know what? Fine. If you want to sit around here, I'll take her to a hospital myself."

Westerly's heart pounded. He couldn't just let Logan and Jack wander back out onto the highway. And even now, a part of him— a dark, hidden, secret part—found itself wondering what Harold would do if Westerly appeared at the university with this dog . . . the dog that could possibly provide the key to stopping this epidemic. Would Harold welcome Westerly back with open arms? Or would he just grab the dog and shut the door in Westerly's face and take all the credit for himself?

But then, these questions might be meaningless. It might already be too late.

"You should know something, Logan," he said. "Taking Jack to the CDC might not even do any good at this point. Your dog may very well be the last healthy dog in Oregon."

Logan's face twisted in disgust. "So what? What about the *people*, Dad? Fifty-six people are already dead from this thing. Maybe more." He raised his eyebrows. "You do read the papers, don't you?"

"I . . ." Westerly swallowed. He hadn't even thought about the people. The rage faded, leaving only a cold void in its place. *What's happening to me?* Logan was right: Westerly was as selfish as a child. He sickened himself.

But Logan didn't have to know about that. Logan didn't have to know about any of Westerly's feelings. Those belonged to him alone. He stood up. "All right. I'll call the university and let them know we're coming."

Logan didn't move. His face was unreadable. "You mean it?"

Westerly nodded. "Yes. I mean it. I want you to get checked out. And we'll see what we can do with your dog."

"You won't take me back to jail?"

"Jail?" Westerly stared at him in surprise. "No. Why?"

"It seems like the kind of thing you would do," Logan said.

Westerly blinked. For some reason, that one remark hurt more than anything Logan had done or said since Westerly had found him.

"To be honest, jail never once crossed my mind, Logan," he replied. "So you can put the dog back down. I'll be ready in just a minute."

WANTED

SEDITION; UNLAWFUL SLAUGHTER OF ANIMALS; UNLAWFUL FLIGHT TO AVOID PROSECUTION

RUDOLPH STAGG

Alias: Rudy Stagg

Date of Birth: December 4, 1960   **Hair:** Brown

Complexion: Dark/Medium   **Eyes:** Brown

Weight: 170–180 pounds   **Height:** 5'10"

Build: Medium   **Sex:** Male

Nationality: U.S.   **Race:** White

Occupation(s): Home security consultant

Scars and Marks: Has a severe dog bite on his left ankle and walks with a limp.

Remarks: Is infected with POS.

CAUTION

RUDOLPH STAGG IS BEING SOUGHT IN CONNECTION WITH THE TRAINING OF ARMED VIGILANTE GROUPS, SEDITION AGAINST THE UNITED STATES OF AMERICA, AND THE UNLAWFUL SHOOTING OF OVER THIRTY DOGS.

HE IS CONSIDERED ARMED AND EXTREMELY DANGEROUS.

IF YOU HAVE ANY INFORMATION CONCERNING THIS PERSON, CONTACT YOUR LOCAL FBI OFFICE.

CHAPTER
TWENTY-ONE

Logan's father was truly amazing. He hadn't said one word since they'd left his house. Not even a peep. In two hours.

Logan knew that he was a so-called nonverbal type himself, but this . . . this was bizarre. Dad *was* aware that Logan was his son, wasn't he? He *did* know that Logan had lived a life for the past seven years, didn't he? A very interesting life, if Logan said so himself—full of groundbreaking inventions and lame Summer Kickoff Barbecues and harrowing escapes from jail and boot camp.

But Dad apparently had no interest in hearing about it. Or in talking about his own life, for that matter.

They were already chugging over the Willamette River into the heart of Portland. The skyscrapers loomed ahead of them, framed against the blue sky as if on a giant postcard. For about the millionth time, Logan glanced over his shoulder at Jack, just to make sure she was still breathing. Yes . . . her chest was rising and falling. So she was alive. She lay there on the backseat, swaddled in a blanket like a newborn. Her eyes were closed.

Logan faced front again. He didn't mind being on the bridge so much because at least he couldn't see any houses. They'd driven past way too many houses on the way to Portland, houses of every kind: old, new, big, small, rich, poor . . . but they all had one thing in common. None of them had dogs in their yards. Not *one*.

On a sunny summer day like today, dogs should be outside. It wasn't right. Logan felt sick whenever they passed a BEWARE OF DOG sign. *What dog?* he wanted to ask. There *were* no dogs.

There were a lot of army trucks, though. And a lot of black ambulances. Which just made Logan feel even sicker. For all he knew, Jack might very well be the last dog alive. If she even survived the rest of the journey . . .

"So, Dad," he said finally. He couldn't stand the silence for another second. He practically had to shout to make himself heard over the rattle of Dad's junk-heap car. "You built that house yourself, huh?"

Dad nodded.

"How long did it take?" Logan asked.

"It's not really done," Dad said. "It's sort of a work in progress. I had help with the heavy stuff. Construction workers did most of the actual building. I just designed it."

"Wow," Logan said. He didn't say it because he was impressed with his father's ingenuity or do-it-yourself gumption. He said it because his father had actually formed real sentences. Several in a row. Incredible.

"So why did you do it?" Logan asked.

Dad's forehead wrinkled. "What do you mean? Why did I build the house?"

"No. Why did you run out on us?"

The question just sort of popped out of Logan's mouth. He hadn't meant to bring up the past. But part of his brain must have figured there was no point in waiting around any longer to ask the question he'd wanted to ask for seven years. After all, they might not have this chance to speak to each other alone again.

"I didn't run out on you," Dad said. "Your mother threw me out."

"That's not the way I heard it," Logan said.

Dad cast a quick sidelong glance at him. "How *did* you hear it?" he asked.

"Actually, I didn't hear anything. I remember that after you got fired from Portland University, you just sat around and did nothing. Mostly, you talked about how mad you were at the guy who fired you. Mom ended up having to pick up your slack. She got fed up. She gave you a choice: Either you go out and get a job, or you go wallow in your own misery somewhere else."

Much to Logan's surprise, Dad nodded. "That's exactly right," he said.

Logan frowned. "It *is*?"

"Yes," Dad said. "Your mother threw me out."

Logan glared at him.

"What?" Dad said.

"Nothing," Logan muttered. He faced forward again.

"You're angry, Logan. Tell me why."

Logan turned to him. "You don't get it. Mom didn't want you to *leave*. She wanted you to shape up."

"She wanted me to shape up, eh?" Dad asked. He smiled.

"What's so funny?"

"Nothing," Dad said. He shrugged as he turned off at the first bridge exit. "Let me ask you something, Logan. Why did your mother send you to boot camp?"

"Because I blew up a microwave oven in a deli," he said.

Dad laughed. "Really?"

"Yeah, really. You think that's funny?"

"No, you just took me by surprise, that's all," Dad said. "Why did you do it?"

"I don't know," Logan mumbled. "A dog was attacking Jack."

Dad didn't say anything for a moment. "I guess you don't want to talk about it."

"Not really." Logan chewed his lip and shifted in his seat. He felt antsy and agitated all of a sudden, as if he'd just chugged a massive cup of coffee. "But you know, it's not what it sounds like," he added. "I mean, I felt bad and all. I would have done something to help make up for it. Robert was just looking for an excuse to get rid of me."

"Oh," Dad said.

"What do you mean, '*oh*'?" Logan snapped.

Dad shrugged again. "Nothing. It's just . . . I believe you. My situation was very similar. Your mother was just looking for an excuse to get rid of *me*."

"No, she wasn't," Logan said.

"How do you know?" Dad asked.

"Because I know Mom. All she wants is for people to do what they're supposed to and for everything to be smooth and organized and . . ." Logan hesitated for a second, searching for the right word.

"Stable?" Dad suggested.

Logan nodded. "Exactly," he said. "Stable."

"Right," Dad said. "That's why she was such a great librarian. She made sure everything was smooth and organized for people who wanted to find books." He glanced at Logan again. "You know, that's how we met. At the Portland University science library. She helped me find a book on Spanish influenza—"

"I *know*, Dad." Logan groaned.

Dad sighed. "What I was saying is, your mother wants more than anything for things to be *stable*," he said. "With a capital *S*. That's why she married Robert."

"You know him?" Logan asked, surprised.

Dad laughed. "Sure. He sold your mother and me our first two cars—didn't you know that? Back then he was at a Toyota dealership, though."

"Whoa." Logan pursed his lips, processing this.

"Anyway, you don't need to know him very well to see he's a stable sort of guy. He works hard to keep everything always the same, all the time. The problem is, *life* isn't stable. But you already know that, Logan. Much better than Robert does, I'd bet."

Logan opened his mouth to answer, or protest, or argue, or—or *something*. But then he closed it. Incredibly enough, Dad was right.

Which meant there really wasn't much point in continuing the conversation. He certainly didn't want to hear any more dumb stories about how Mom used to find Dad books. Besides, the silence wasn't really so bad.

Something was very, very wrong in Portland.

Logan wasn't sure what, exactly (or maybe he just didn't want to think too hard about it), but the prickling anxiety he'd felt since they'd gotten off the bridge was slowly turning to fear. There was hardly any traffic. Most of the streets were blocked off with police barricades. His father had pretty much been driving in circles for the past twenty minutes. The university was less than half a mile from the river, but they couldn't seem to get within four blocks of it. And they kept passing the same groups of people in those billowy safe suits, huddled on street corners or in doorways . . . or at least, Logan assumed they were the same groups of people. It was impossible to tell.

He glanced back at Jack. Her breathing was more strained. Her throat kept making a weird rattling noise. Logan's jaw tightened.

Now *he* was having a hard time breathing. The hospital was close. He could see the north tower.

Okay, worst-case scenario: He would grab Jack and jump out of the car and hurdle the barricades, and, yes, maybe the guys in the safe suits would try to stop him . . . but he would simply barrel right past them and straight into the emergency room because their plastic was so slick that they wouldn't be able to get a grip on him, anyway—

The car jerked to a stop.

"Uh-oh," Dad muttered.

Logan faced forward again. "What?"

But his father didn't have time to answer. The car was surrounded by a furious, screaming, red-faced mob. Instinctively, Logan slammed his fist down on the lock and backed so far away from the door that he practically crawled into his father's lap. The people seemed to appear out of nowhere, like a swarm of bees. Their voices buzzed; their enraged faces pressed against the windows. And all their anger seemed to be directed at Logan and his father. The weirdest thing about it was that Logan felt mildly guilty. In spite of his terror, he felt as if he were a famous criminal who was being escorted to a court-house and forced to confront his victims. And he shouldn't have. He was just trying to get his dog fixed. He didn't understand what was going on. Were all these people sick? Were things really that bad?

"Wh-what's going on?" he stammered.

"This must be the only the way to the hospital," Dad mumbled.

Before Logan could ask another question, his father grabbed the gearshift and gunned the engine. The next thing Logan knew, his body was slammed back against the door. The car swerved around a corner. The hospital swam into view. Logan winced as he stared out the window. People were diving out of the way of the car. Dad didn't slow down. He didn't try to hit anyone, but he wasn't exactly avoiding anyone, either. Logan stopped breathing. His limbs froze. *This is crazy. This can't be happening. This can't be . . .*

The car screeched to a halt again, and Logan's face nearly slammed against the dashboard.

"Stop right there!" somebody barked.

Logan looked up. A pale, beefy security guard in a blue uniform was blocking their path, clutching a rifle. He must have weighed close to three hundred pounds. He leaned forward and glared angrily through the windshield.

All at once, his brow furrowed. His face softened a bit.

"Dr. Westerly?" he called. "Is that you?"

Dad nodded. He rolled down his window. "How are you, Phil?" he asked.

"Well, not great, as you can see," the guard said. He hurried around to the driver's side. "We've been waiting for you. Sorry about this mess."

"How long has the situation been like this?" Dad asked.

The guard shook his head. "A few days now."

Logan glanced from Dad to the guard. For some reason, they seemed to be taking their time to get reacquainted, which seemed to Logan a very dumb idea. From his perspective, it would be a good idea to roll the window back up. Soon. *Immediately.*

"What's going on?" somebody in the mob screamed.

"Back off!" the guard shouted, waving his gun at them.

Dad's fingers danced on the steering wheel. "Quite a scene out here," he said.

"You could say that." The guard bent back down by the window. "It's getting harder and harder to handle—" He broke off suddenly.

"What is it?" Dad asked.

The guard shook his head, his eyes widening. "Is that a *dog* in the back of your car?"

"Yes, it's my son's. I let Harold Marks know that I was coming with her—"

"Dr. Marks didn't mention that part to me," the guard interrupted. His voice trembled "Look, you'd better get going. There's National Guardsmen all over the place. They've been killing dogs." He backed away from the car. "Straight through into the garage. Dr. Marks is waiting for you. He made sure your old space was waiting for you, too."

Dad laughed. "Isn't that nice," he said. He didn't move, even though the mob was closing in again.

Logan frowned at him. If he'd thought Robert should win first prize for Freak of the Year, Dad was Freak Champion of the World. He was in a completely different category. Ultrafreak. Megafreak. There wasn't even a word for it.

"Uh, Dad?" Logan growled. "I hate to spoil your fun, but my dog might get shot if we stick around out here. So I think we should go."

"I guess you're right," Dad said. But he didn't sound as though he meant it.

CHAPTER
TWENTY-TWO

The scene inside the hospital was even weirder than the scene on the streets. Normally, hospitals were quiet. Almost *eerily* quiet. Not this one. This hospital was a madhouse. Logan had never seen anything like it. He clutched Jack tightly in his arms as his father led him through a maze of brightly lit corridors—all of which were crawling with figures in safe suits, angry-looking doctors and nurses, and an occasional patient. None of them seemed to have any idea what to do with themselves except shout at each other . . . except, of course, when Logan walked past them. Then they all shut up and gaped at Jack.

Logan's back was beginning to hurt from Jack's weight. Jack's breathing was getting worse. Every time Logan took another step, she made a strange gurgling noise—as if she were rinsing her mouth out with mouthwash. She kept coughing and panting. "It's going to be okay, girl," Logan whispered to her.

He hoped he was telling the truth.

Dr. Marks's big, plush office was empty. It stayed empty.

Logan didn't get it. Out on the street, the guard had said that Dr. Marks would be waiting for *them*. But ten minutes had already ticked by with agonizing slowness, and Dr. Marks was still nowhere to be seen.

Dad hadn't said a word. He'd just handed Logan a plastic cup of water for Jack, then sat down on the giant leather couch and stared at all the framed diplomas and awards on the wall. Occasionally, he sneered. Maybe he was having a conversation with himself in his head.

Logan tried to get Jack to drink from the cup, but as it turned out, she wasn't thirsty. Or maybe she just was physically unable to drink. She lay sprawled on the floor, her breath rasping in her chest. And Logan couldn't do anything about it. He really wished he could find one of those National Guardsmen everybody kept talking about and maybe borrow a grenade or five and blow up a bathroom or something—because then the idiots might finally understand that some people actually wanted their dogs to survive.

"So, Dad," Logan said. "Where do you think this guy is?"

"No doubt doing something very important," Dad replied.

Logan blinked. Well. There was another totally whacked-out answer. So much for the relatively normal conversation they'd had in the car. Logan decided he would just stop asking questions. He tossed the cup in the garbage, then sat beside Jack on the thick beige rug and stroked the back of her neck, teasing gently at her shredded and blood-caked fur. Every once in a while, she twitched. Her eyes were rheumy and gummed up.

"Don't worry, girl," he said. "We're going to get help soon."

"I hope that's true," Dad said. "I really do."

The door opened. A man in a white lab coat stepped into the office. He quickly shut the door behind him and locked it. He was wearing neatly pressed suit pants and a tie. They swished in the way that only really expensive clothes do. His shirt had cuff links. His hair was slicked back with gel, like Mr. Wallace's hair. But what struck Logan most about him was how drawn and tired his face looked. The circles under his eyes were like bruises.

"Craig," he said. His tone was blank. "Sorry to keep you waiting."

Logan stood up. He figured that was the polite thing to do. Not Dad. He kept sitting.

"Hello, Harold," Dad said.

Neither of them said a word after that.

Logan waited. Jack whined.

"Are you Dr. Marks?" Logan asked.

"Yes." The man offered Logan a brittle smile and extended a hand. Logan shook it. "And you must be Craig's son. Logan?"

"Yeah, and now that we've all met, can you please help my dog?" Logan demanded.

Dr. Marks stopped smiling. He turned to Dad. "A chip off the old block, I see," he said.

"If you want to say something to Logan, you can address him directly," Dad said. "He's a human being. He's right in front of you."

"I see that."

Logan glanced fom one to the other. His breathing quickened. He felt like taking their heads in either hand and smashing them together like two bowling balls—*crack!*—but that would be fairly dumb, seeing as they were the only ones who could possibly help Jack.

"Um, can you guys talk about me later? In case you haven't noticed, there's a dog on the rug. And she's dying."

Dr. Marks sighed. He knelt beside Jack and gave her a quick once-over. He acted as if he were examining a piece of meat. "So you claim that this dog is immune to POS," he said.

"She is immune," Dad said. "Her tissue shows no signs of astrogliosis. She was attacked by a dog with POS, and—" He hesitated. "By the way, who came up with the name psychotic outburst syndrome? It was you, wasn't it?"

Dr. Marks pulled a pair of surgical gloves from his lab coat pocket. "It's an appropriate name," he said. He blew into each glove, inflating them like balloons, then slipped them on. "I assume you found traces of astrogliosis in the attacker's tissue."

"Yes."

"What about blood toxicity?"

"The sample spoke for itself. None of her proteins contained amyloid rods."

"I doubt that, but never mind," Dr. Marks muttered. He lifted one of Jack's ears, holding it delicately in his fingertips. "Has she had her vaccines? DAAPL dash CPV?"

"As far as I know," Dad said dryly. "She's not my dog."

"The absence of astrogliosis doesn't necessarily guarantee immunity," Dr. Marks said. "Spongiform change can manifest itself . . ."

Logan stopped listening. He couldn't understand a word of what they were saying. Not that it mattered, anyway. It was obvious that this conversation had nothing to do with the actual words that were coming out of their mouths. It had to do with their tone, with the way they refused to make eye contact. This conversation wasn't about Jack's condition or weird medical terms or POS; it was about *them*—their problems, whatever they were. They were just disguising it with their scientific jargon so they could pretend they were being adult and professional.

And they weren't helping Jack at all.

Come to think of it, the whole thing reminded Logan of the way he and Devon Wallace talked to each other. Devon was always trying to prove how smart he was, and Logan was always trying to show him that he didn't really care. It was pretty much exactly the same, actually. Dr. Marks was the Devon Wallace character in this scenario—the perfect one, the rich one, the one with all the *stuff*, the awards—and, sad to say, Dad was Logan . . . angry, impatient, and, in the end, unable to figure out why being perfect mattered so much.

". . . need to move her," Dr. Marks was saying. "We need to get her to intensive care if she's going to have any hope of survival. There's fluid in her lungs."

"Then move her," Dad said.

Dr. Marks glanced up from Jack. "Not without a safe suit. I'm not taking any chances."

"But you just touched her ears," Dad said.

"I'm not going to get into an argument over this, Craig," Dr. Marks said in a toneless voice. "Maybe you've forgotten what it's like to work in a professional environment. That's understandable. But—"

The doorknob rattled.

Dr. Marks rolled his eyes. "Yes?" he called.

Somebody knocked. "Harold Marks?" a man answered. "Is that you?"

"Yes." Dr. Marks frowned. "Who's there? Can I help you?"

"Security. We have a situation out here."

"Not again." Dr. Marks groaned. He stood and unlocked the door. It flew open, nearly knocking him over.

Logan flinched. A grizzled man in a black hat stumbled into the room. He didn't look like a security guard. He wasn't wearing a uniform. He was dressed all in black except for a bloody homemade bandage around his left ankle. He slammed the door.

"Who are you?" Dr. Marks said in a loud voice. "What on earth are you doing?"

The man raised a shaky finger to his lips. "Shhh," he whispered.

He stood on his right foot, wobbling. With his other hand, he reached behind his back.

A second later, his hand reappeared—only this time it was holding a gun. A big one. With a silencer. He pointed it at Dr. Marks.

Logan blinked.

There's a guy with a gun in here.

He could feel his heart beating. The sound was far away, though. It was as if his body had sprung a leak. Every single drop of blood felt as if it were draining out of him.

He glanced at his father. Dad was sitting perfectly still, his eyes fixed on the gun.

"I'm Rudy Stagg," the man said.

Rudy Stagg. Logan swallowed. He'd heard that name before. But where?

"Recognize my name?" Rudy Stagg asked.

Dr. Marks nodded very rapidly. "Yes . . . yes, I—uh, I suppose I do," he stammered. "What, ah, what can I do for you, Mr. Stagg?"

"I'm the famous dog killer," Rudy Stagg said. "I'm a wanted man." He limped over to the couch and sat on the armrest, keeping his gun aimed squarely at Dr. Marks. "And now I'm a sick man, too. I got bit by a dog. Did you get my e-mails?" Before Dr. Marks could reply, he snarled, "I know you got them, you jerk, even though you never replied."

Logan's head swam. *The famous dog killer.* So. This man Rudy Stagg killed dogs. And he had a gun. And he was inside this office. Not three feet from Jack.

Jack whined.

Rudy Stagg jerked at the sound.

His shoulder started twitching. He stared at Jack. A drop of drool fell from his lips and landed on his jeans.

Logan wobbled on his feet. His stomach turned. He was worried he might puke.

"What's that?" Rudy Stagg hissed.

"That's a dog," Dr. Marks said.

"It's a dog that can help you," Dad said, speaking up for the first time. "If you're sick, this dog can—"

"You can't see me because you're seeing a *dog*?" Rudy Stagg interrupted, whirling back toward Dr. Marks.

"It's not that," Dr. Marks said. "It's that—"

"Shut up!" Rudy Stagg shouted, glaring at him. The pistol wavered. "Dogs are what got us into this mess. Don't you know anything? Dogs are what made *me* sick."

"Please," Dad said. He leaned forward. "Listen. This dog is immune. We're going to use her to create a medicine that can cure you—"

"I said *shut up*! Do you think I'm stupid? Huh? Do you think I don't know what you're planning, all of you people with your fancy suits and your black helicopters?"

Logan's eyes widened. Stagg wasn't just a little weird. He was a lunatic.

"Mr. Stagg, please," Dr. Marks said. "That's the illness talking. Let us help you—"

"Shut up," Stagg said again, though more quietly. He sighted down the barrel of the pistol at Dr. Marks, whose face turned the color of moldy cheese. Then, suddenly, Stagg turned his pistol on Jack. "You know, I thought I'd done my very last dog job. But I got time for one more. Yes, sir."

He cocked the hammer.

Time came to a standstill.

Logan saw it all before him with weird clarity. Rudy Stagg was going to shoot Jack. Rudy Stagg was going to put an end to Dad and Dr. Marks's stupid argument because there would be no point in arguing anymore, because there would be no cure—because Jack would be dead. And if that were to happen, Logan really didn't see much point in hanging around this lame planet anymore. It was just going to get a whole lot lamer, a whole lot quicker.

He dove on top of Jack's body.

"Logan, no!" Dad yelled. "Don't—"

Logan heard a soft *thwip*, like the sound of a rubber band. There was a sharp stinging in his back. It burned. Man, how it burned! Warm wetness spread over the front of his sweatshirt. Out of the corner of his eye, he saw blood pooling on the expensive beige carpet.

Now it was getting hard to breathe. Logan opened his mouth, but he couldn't seem to suck in air. Shadows closed in around the edges of his vision. He was dimly aware of yelling and footsteps and the door flying open and a bunch of other garbage . . . but it was funny to him because it didn't really matter. Jack was beneath him. She was safe. He tried to laugh, but he ended up falling asleep instead.

The spaceship was hard to steer. Logan clutched the control stick, but it felt heavy and supersluggish. A meteor shower was coming. Pretty soon he'd be right in the thick of it. He was nervous; he couldn't remember if he'd ever flown this spaceship before—but for some reason, it was weirdly familiar.

Actually, he was pretty sure he'd built it. Or at least designed it. He knew where everything was: the hyperdrive button, the tractor beam, and most especially the Logan Moore Torpedo of Ultimate Destruction (LMTUD)—a weapon that was no bigger than a pencil but could instantly reduce any enemy to a small green stain.

Jack sat beside him in the copilot's seat. She kept trying to stick her head out the window. Her tail wagged and wagged.

Logan giggled. "You can't stick your head out the window," he said. "There's no air out there. We're in outer space."

Now that he noticed it, he was having a tough time breathing himself. Was there a leak somewhere? He wasn't wearing a helmet. He knew he should be wearing one, but he wasn't. Whatever. There wasn't any time.

Pow! The first meteor bounced against the ship.

Logan nearly fell out of his seat. Jack barked. Logan regained his balance, deftly maneuvering the control stick. He swerved in and out among the rocks, missing most of them but bouncing against some like a marble in a pinball machine. Then, all at once, he was out of the meteor shower . . . and he could see one last big space rock—more like an asteroid than a meteor—dead ahead. Jack barked at it. Her eyes flashed to him. He knew she wanted him to go there.

He frowned.

There were three little figures in space suits standing on the rocky surface. They were all waving at him frantically with both hands.

Logan tapped the brakes. The ship slowed down a little.

Hey . . . one of those guys was Perry, the jerk from the Blue Mountain Camp for Boys. Logan could see his pale face. The ship was very close now. And the little shrimp next to him was Sergeant Bell. Ha! In his tiny space suit, Sergeant Bell looked like a midget. And the third one . . . Was that Robert?

Weird. Maybe they'd all gone on a field trip together.

Logan was hovering right over them now. They looked scared. They must have been marooned out here.

Jack barked again. Her ears flattened. She growled—then stopped.

Logan reached for the LMTUD trigger. Die, scumbags!

But then he looked at Jack. Her eyes were soft. And right then, he changed his mind. He would not turn his enemies into small green stains. He would suck them up into the ship with his tractor beam and save them. He was bigger than them and better than them, and he would show them mercy—because that was the right thing to do, the thing that they would never do, small-minded fools that they were.

True, they all belonged on his Things I Hate list. But looking at them now, stranded out there, Logan could only feel sorry for them.

Yes, it was better to help them. Maybe they would learn something from this. Who goes on a field trip in the middle of outer space?

The tractor beam sucked them right up into the cockpit: poof!

They all clung to each other as Logan pulled away from the asteroid and sped off into the vast, starry blackness. They hugged each other like babies.

"Thanks for saving us," Robert said. "But don't you think Jack should get down from that chair? I don't want her getting in the habit of—"

Jack barked at him.

Robert didn't say anything after that.

Logan smiled and shrugged. He reached over and patted Jack on the head. She really was a much better girl than Robert ever gave her credit for.

PART VI
AUGUST 18-21

CHAPTER TWENTY-THREE

At first, there was nothing but bright white light and softness.

Every single time I wake up, I have no idea where I am.

Logan wondered if he'd somehow ended up back at his father's place. But then he sniffed the air. Something was different. It smelled . . . *metallic.* He blinked a few times. His back hurt. He tried to swallow. His throat was incredibly dry. And incredibly sore.

Fuzzy shapes hovered in the air above him. It took him a moment to realize that they were two heads. One on the left, one on the right. And the bright light was a big light bulb in the center of a silver dish—right in the middle of them.

"He's awake," the head on the right said.

Robert?

Logan squinted up at him. It was Robert, all right. There was no mistaking that craggy, pock-marked face.

"What . . . what's going on?" Logan croaked. He sounded like a frog.

"You're in the hospital, sweetie," the other head said.

Mom. Logan's pulse quickened. The other head belonged to Mom. But she never called him "sweetie" unless something was wrong. He heard the faint sound of a machine beeping. The beeping grew faster.

"What happened?" he asked.

"You got shot," Robert said. "The bullet collapsed one of your lungs. You've been under for three weeks."

Logan blinked. He couldn't quite grasp what Robert was telling him.

"But you're all right now," Mom added. "They called us this morning and told us you'd woken up briefly." A watery smile tugged at the corner of her lips. "You were asleep again by the time we got here, though."

Logan closed his eyes, struggling to remember. A series of images whirled his mind, a tornado of them—but they were blurry and distorted, like headlights passing on a rainy highway. He saw the panicked crowd outside the university, the expression on his father's face when he talked to that jerk of a doctor . . . but most clearly of all, that freak with the gun. Right. *Rudy Stagg*. The "famous dog-killer." He'd tried to shoot Jack, but Logan dove on top of her.

I got shot.

Logan opened his eyes again.

The faces of Mom and Robert were still floating above him, like two planets in outer space. Maybe he was still dreaming. There was no way he could have been shot. . . .

He bit down on his cheek.

Ouch. That hurt.

So he was awake. And he wasn't dead. Everything must have turned out all right, because he was *here*—in a hospital bed, hooked up to a bunch of different machines. There was a tube in his arm. There was even a tube up his nose. Man, was that irritating. Still, he found himself grinning, in spite of his discomfort. *Wow.* This . . . this was pretty wild. He had actually been *shot*. Not even a guy like

Perry could say that. He doubted even if Sergeant Bell could say that, and he'd been in a war. It was sort of cool, in a way.

"Where's Jack?" Logan croaked.

Mom and Robert exchanged a glance.

"What?" Logan said.

"I'm, uh . . ." Robert cleared his throat. "I'm going to go get some coffee, okay? Logan, do you want anything?"

Do I want anything? Alarm bells instantly went off in his brain. Being called "sweetie" was one thing . . . but now Robert was offering to be his valet? Logan stared at him. The pain in his chest suddenly seemed detached, remote. The machine beeped away, faster and faster.

"Logan, I have to tell you something," Mom said. Robert hesitated on the doorway.

"Where's Jack?" Logan demanded again.

"At a research facility."

Logan blinked. "A . . . what?"

Mom nodded, biting her lip. "Logan, she's—well, she's at the CDC headquarters downtown. With your father. She isn't well."

"What do you mean?"

"She's on life support," Mom said. "You see . . . she was more hurt than you probably realized. When you brought her to the hospital, she was already in very, very bad shape—"

"So she's alive, right?" Logan interrupted.

Mom swallowed. "Her heart is beating, yes," she said after a moment. "But she can't breathe on her own. She can't feed herself. You see, after. . . . after everything happened in Dr. Marks's office, they rushed her to one of the emergency rooms. That was when they finally realized that your father was right all along; she *is* immune to POS. So they're keeping her alive to study her, to use her tissue to help make an antidote, because she was the only dog in the world they could find, *your* dog . . ." The words came tumbling out of Mom's mouth in a rush. But then just as quickly, they stopped, as if a plug had been pulled. She exhaled. "Jack isn't going to make it, Logan. I'm sorry."

Logan shook his head. This wasn't making any sense. "What do you mean?" he asked.

"They're going to have to put her to sleep, sweetie. They have no choice."

"You just said they were keeping her alive," he said.

Mom looked at Robert, still standing in the doorway.

"They *are* keeping her alive," Robert said. "You saved her. But her injuries were just too much. She was beaten too badly. She's . . . uh, she's not going to get better."

Logan turned his head to gaze at Robert. The pain in his chest was completely gone now. He felt numb, as if his body had been dipped in ice.

Robert cleared his throat. "See, you saved her from that crazy guy who would have killed her right here in this hospital." He looked at the floor. "And the good news is, they got him. He didn't hurt anybody else after that. He was wanted by the FBI, if you can believe it. But, um, he . . . uh, he's dead now. He died of POS in jail."

The good news? The shock at having survived a gunshot wound flew from Logan's mind, leaving only a red haze in its place. A guy had *died*, and that was good news?

Come to think of it, lots of people had died. And Jack was going to die, too. Diving in front of that bullet might have saved her for the time being—but apparently, it still wasn't good enough. Logan started to tremble. He could see Jack as if she were right in front of him: the way she dug up Robert's lawn, the way she peed on Robert's bathroom floor—the way she flew out of the woods and into Logan's arms when he thought he'd never see her again.

Now she was going to die.

Okay, okay, she wasn't dead yet. There had to be *some* hope. Dad was a good scientist. Wasn't he? She was under top care. She was still alive. She was badly hurt—unconscious, maybe—but *alive*. Logan squirmed under the covers. A hot ball of angry fire formed deep inside him. It started rising . . . rising up through his chest and into his throat and hitting his face and punching through— and all of a sudden, it exploded in a burst of tears.

To his horror, he found himself sobbing uncontrollably.

What am I doing? He had to stop. *Stop. Stop. Stop.* He hated himself. He hadn't even wanted a stupid dog in the first place because the stupid dog was a stupid punishment handed down by the All-Knowing Dictator of Everything . . . and crying was pathetic and certainly not fitting for a master inventor or a fugitive from the law or a runaway. *Not at all.* But he cried so hard that he couldn't even catch his breath. And Mom and Robert just stood there, watching him. As if he were on display. As if he were some pathetic crying kid on a TV show.

He hadn't cried since he was seven years old.

"I'm so sorry, Logan," Mom breathed. She stroked his hair with a tentative hand. "I'm so sorry."

"Don't," Logan choked out, brushing her hand away. His voice was thick. He sniffed and fought to control himself. "It's all right." He drew in a couple of deep, shaky breaths. *Relax.* He was pretty sure that no more tears were coming—at least not right now. But that hot ball of fire was still there, still right behind his face. He could feel it.

Robert cleared his throat again. "Well, I . . . um, I'm going to go get that coffee," he said. "Visiting hours are almost up." His eyes flashed to Logan, then back to the floor. He took a deep breath. "Look, Logan, I just wanted you to know that . . ." He shook his head. "I don't know. I just wanted to make sure you were okay."

Logan stared at him. *Make sure I'm okay.* That might have been the stupidest thing Robert had ever said. Which, in a lifetime of stupidity, was a pretty impressive feat. But for once, Logan wasn't all that annoyed. Maybe it was because he was too angry and confused and miserable to be annoyed. Or maybe it was just that the All-Knowing Dictator of Everything had admitted something he never had before: "I don't know." Now *that* was impressive. It didn't even matter that Logan had no idea what Robert was talking about. *Robert* didn't seem to have any idea what he was talking about—which meant that those three words must have been pretty tough for him to say. In fact, Logan actually felt sort of *bad* for the guy . . . the way he was just hovering by the bed with this strange, almost pleading look on his face. For a second, he almost wanted to reach out and pat Robert on the back.

"Thanks, Robert," Logan said. "I'll be fine."

Robert nodded. A strained smile crossed his face. "Hey, I meant to tell you," he said. "Remember that remote control thing you made? It's come in pretty handy these past few weeks. I don't lose the remote anymore. I . . . uh, I guess I should thank you. As soon as you're better, you can show me how to work it the right way."

He slunk out of the room, closing the door behind him.

Logan glanced at Mom.

"He's trying, Logan," she whispered. "He really is."

"So when can I go to the CDC Headquarters?" he asked.

Mom sniffed. "Logan, I think—"

Somebody knocked on the door.

"Yes?" Mom called.

A nurse stepped into the room. She smiled apologetically at Mom. "I'm sorry, ma'am," she said. "But visiting hours are over."

Mom nodded, blinking a few times. For a second, Logan wondered if she was going to cry. "I . . . I'll see you tomorrow, okay?" she whispered. She bent over and kissed him on the forehead, then hurried from the room.

The nurse smiled at Logan and shut the door.

Logan slumped back against his pillows.

For a long time, he lay still, groggily staring at the ceiling, struggling to sort out his thoughts. Why couldn't he go see Jack right now? What was the problem? They could take him there in an ambulance, couldn't they? His own *father* was working there, right? It was ridiculous. It *stank*. There was so much he wanted to know, that he had a *right* to know. . . .

He really wished that nurse hadn't booted his mom out of here.

He really wished a lot of things, actually.

Well, maybe that wasn't quite true. When it came down to it, he pretty much had only one wish. He wished he were still unconscious. That way, he would still be with Jack.

CHAPTER
TWENTY-FOUR

After three days of lying in bed—still hooked to all those different machines, with all those annoying tubes still jammed up his nostrils—Logan had a strange realization. He'd already watched more TV in this hospital, total, than he had in his entire life up until this point. It was kind of amazing.

Well, either that or pitiful. Or both.

Of course, it wasn't entirely his fault. The nurse on the day shift, Nurse Williams (who was really nice, in spite of the fact that she talked to Logan as if he were three) seemed to believe that he wanted the TV on at all times. She never asked if he wanted to do anything else. She seemed incapable of believing that a fourteen-year-old would want to do anything *besides* watch TV all day.

The interesting part was that Logan was starting to understand why she might think that—or more to the point, why so many people (Robert, for instance) spent so much time in front of the tube instead of, say, reading. Reading required actual *concentration*. If you skipped a paragraph, or even an important sentence, you could lose the entire story. With most TV shows, though, you didn't have to concentrate at all. You could space out for a good ten minutes, then come back and still figure out what was going on.

And that was a good thing, as far as Logan was concerned. At the moment, his concentration was completely shot.

He continued to stare blankly at the screen. It was a rerun of some ancient cop show. (That was another thing: at every hour of every day—even at 3 pm on a Saturday—you could always find a rerun of an ancient cop show.) As usual, there was a car chase. This episode was about how some rich guy had been murdered by his wife . . . or something. Logan was paying even less attention than usual.

Every few seconds, his eyes would drift over to the brand new set of *How-To-Build Electronics* books that Robert had bought for him yesterday. They sat untouched in a neat stack on top of his tray table, not two feet away. He really should crack one open. Then maybe he'd figure out how to build a miniature bionic lung so he could get out of this stupid bed and away from these dumb machines and be done with it.

But he didn't look at the books.

It wasn't just that he wouldn't be able to concentrate on them. It was that every time he glanced at them, his stomach kept twisting into a knot, and his brain kept producing a bunch of thoughts that he didn't want to deal with.

First, he thought about how truly shocking it was that Robert had done something nice for him. And not just *anything* nice, not just an offhand gesture, but something thoughtful and cool—and, in a symbolic sort of way, perfectly apologetic for all the lame things he'd done in the past, like taking away the books in the first place. Then he thought about all the other things that Robert done for him: getting him the baseball mitt, sending him to boot camp . . . and all *that*, of course, made him think about Jack. And then the hot ball of fire would start to rise and he would grit his teeth and the machine's beeping would get faster and louder. . . .

Stop it.

Logan wrenched his eyes back to the TV set.

At the very least, he could write Robert a thank-you note. That would kill some time. It wouldn't take a whole lot of concentration, either.

Dear Robert, Thanks for the books. I mean it. Mom says you're trying, and I know that she's right, and I really appreciate it, and blah, blah, blah.

The standard thank-you note stuff. After that, he would—

"Your pet deserves the best!" a voice blared from the screen.

Logan flinched. He hadn't even noticed, but the cop show had cut to a cat-food commercial. Some woman who looked and sounded uncannily like Mrs. Dougherty from the animal shelter was snuggling with a little black cat. Right there. Right in front of his face.

Your pet deserves the best!

This was all wrong. Bad. Unwatchable. Logan fumbled for the remote and thrust it toward the screen, jabbing blindly at the buttons with his thumb.

The volume rose.

Logan's breath quickened. "Come on," he hissed. "Come on—"

There was a knock on the door.

"Logan? It's Nurse Williams."

"Okay!" he yelled automatically. The hot ball of fire was raging inside his body once more. His eyes darted to the remote and zeroed in on the power button. He grasped the remote with both hands and punched the button as hard as he could. The TV winked off just as Nurse Williams entered the room.

Logan glanced up at her. His heart was still racing.

He frowned. He couldn't even see her face. It was obscured by a massive floral arrangement.

"Look what I have," she said in a happy, sing-song voice. "*Look-what-I-ha-aah-ave.*"

Logan gulped. He had no idea how to respond. The machine beeped away.

"Where shall I put them?" she asked.

"Uh . . . anywhere," he finally managed. He shook his head, peering at the dizzying array of colors. "Are those for me?"

Nurse Williams laughed. "Of course they are," she said, setting the flowers down on the hospital dresser. "Oh, doesn't that just brighten up the room? Some of your fans want to show their support."

Logan wrinkled his forehead. "Some of my . . . fans?" he asked. *It must be Dad,* he thought. Of course. Apparently, Dad had been trying to call him several times a day, but every time he rang up, Logan was either asleep or getting examined. So this must be his way of saying sorry. Logan almost chuckled. Leave it his father to be clueless enough to send Logan *flowers.*

"It's from the Wallace family, " Nurse Williams said. She plucked a card from inside the pot and handed it to Logan.

His smile faded. *The Wallace family?*

"I'll leave your other mail on your tray, all right?" Nurse Williams said. She set down a small stack of cards and envelopes on top of the electronics books, then patted Logan on the head and left the room.

Logan blinked at the card. He wasn't sure which emotion was stronger: disappointment that his father *still* hadn't managed to get in touch with him, or disbelief that the Wallace family had sent him flowers. Best not to think about it, probably. He tore open the envelope.

The front of the card was blank, except for the words *Get Well Soon* embossed in gold lettering. Inside, there were two notes. The one on top was from Devon's parents.

Dear Logan,
    Just wanted to let you know we're thinking of you and praying for a speedy recovery.
                    All Best,
                    Mr. and Mrs. Wallace

The other was from Devon himself.

Hey Logan,
    I thought you might want to know that you're becoming a big celebrity around the neighborhood. Everybody asks me about Jack. I tell them that she dug out of your basement and ran forty miles to find you, which is the coolest thing ever. It's weird, because talking about your dog makes me feel a little better about my dog. I know that probably doesn't make a lot of sense. Otis died of POS three weeks ago. I guess I'm still kind of messed up about it. Anyway, I'm sorry I called Jack weird on the street that day.
                    Your friend,
                    Devon

Once again, Logan felt a peculiar knot in his stomach. He didn't know if he could take any more surprises. He'd always assumed Devon Wallace was an idiot. Devon Wallace had always *acted* like an idiot. But this . . . this was not the note Logan would ever dream Devon could write in a million years. Somehow, Devon managed to touch on what really *was* the coolest thing ever: that Jack had defied all odds and risked her life just to be with Logan. They were more than just dog-owner and dog. They were partners. And Devon understood that.

The card began to tremble in Logan's fingers. He dropped it on the tray table. He knew he shouldn't think about Jack, but he couldn't help it. *He* should dig out of this hospital room and run away to be by her side. She brought out surprises in everyone: Robert, Mom . . . even Devon Wallace, somebody who barely knew her. But Logan understood why. Because when *he'd* been with Jack, he'd always surprised himself, too. He'd become somebody else, somebody better than the person he was by himself.

Only now did he realize it. Only now, while Jack was on life-support.

Logan swallowed and shook his head. Weird: His mood was crappy; he was on the verge of crying; he had plastic tubes up his nose; he was bedridden—but Devon Wallace had actually made him feel pretty good for a brief second. Now *that* was something he shouldn't think too hard about. At least not now. But maybe when he got back home, he would let Devon whip his butt in pong-pong.

Sighing, he reached for the envelope on the top of the pile. It, too, was plain white. There was no return address. He opened it and pulled out a letter.

Dear Logan,

I gave up trying to call, because you always seem to be asleep when I do. I know you need lots of rest, so I figured I'd write to you. This way, I can also think about what I really want to say.

First off, I hope you're feeling okay, in spite of everything that's happened. The doctor says that with some physical therapy, you'll be as good as new. But you know about doctors. After all, your old man's a doctor, and look at the way he turned out . . .

That was a joke.

I probably shouldn't be joking around right now. There isn't much to joke about. But I think anything that can make us laugh or smile is a good thing.

Logan, I know that you've heard about Jack's condition. And I know there's nothing I can do or say that will make you feel any better about it. I know, because I think about my own dog every single day. It's hard to describe. I've never been good with words. But every time I go for a walk, my hand feels empty, because there's no leash in it. And every time I sit down to eat, I lose my appetite because Jasmine isn't waiting for me to give her the scraps.

So I just want you to know, if you ever feel the same way, you won't be alone. You can even talk to me about it.

I want you to know something else, too. Because of what you did, we were able to keep Jack alive. That bullet would have killed her for sure.

But I also have a confession to make: I was angry with you for jumping in front of that gun. I was angry because if I had lost you, I'd never be able to tell you how proud you make me. You're honest and brave—two qualities that are generally in pretty short supply on this planet.

Anyway, we're going to keep Jack on life-support until you come and say good-bye to her. That's a promise. I've been working with Dr. Marks and the CDC to use her cells to create a treatment for POS. It's going to take a while longer, but things are looking very positive. I truly believe that soon, thanks to

Jack, we'll put an end to this disease once and for all.

You deserve a lot of the credit for this, too. This was your dog. This was the dog that you chose and loved and cared for and fought for until the very end. You saved her life, and as a result, I think you're going to save a lot of other lives, as well— both dogs and people.

There's no quick fix. But there's hope for a cure.

I guess that's all for now. I'll see you as soon as you're well enough.

Love,

Dad

P.S. Mom was right about me. So were you. But I'm trying.

Logan folded the letter and put it back in the envelope. A tear fell from his cheek and splashed on the paper.

There's no quick fix.

No, there never was. Dad had been right in the car that day: life wasn't stable. It was about as far from stable as you could get. Life was a rickety old spaceship in the middle of a meteor storm, bouncing around and getting smashed and making you feel like you were going to puke, and you just had to hold onto your fellow astronauts and try to make it through, because that was the only choice you had.

Which meant that maybe trying was enough. Or not.

But in the end, trying was really all you could ask a person to do.

EPILOGUE

OCTOBER 5

Article published on page 1 of *The Redmont Daily Standard*, October 5

"JACK" LAID TO REST
CANINE RESPONSIBLE FOR POS CURE
BURIED AT HER HOME
By Sheila Davis

NEWBURG, OR, October 5—Jack, the only dog ever proven to be immune to POS (psychotic outburst syndrome), whose cell tissue was used in the recent development of an experimental POS antidote and vaccine, died Thursday night at a CDC research facility in Portland. She was approximately a year old.

Jack became internationally famous in the wake of the POS epidemic after it was discovered she could not be infected with the disease.

A wild mix of a variety of dog breeds, Jack was picked up by the ASPCA in June of this year, wandering on Route 78 just outside of Newburg. She was brought to the Newburg animal shelter.

"To be honest, we didn't think we'd ever find a home for her," Ruth Dougherty, the director of the shelter, stated. "She was just too wild. And not friendly at all."

Fourteen-year-old Logan Moore, however, apparently saw past her less than desirable personality traits. He insisted on adopting her, in spite of warnings from Ms. Dougherty and other employees of the shelter.

"It was pretty amazing to see them together," Logan's mother, Marianne Moore, said in a recent interview. "Jack